THE STONY POINT DIRECTORATE

MIKE KONYU

Copyright © 2023 Mike Konyu
All rights reserved.

No part of this publication may be reproduced, stored in a retrieval system, or transmitted, in any form or by any means, electronic, mechanical, photocopying, recording, or otherwise, without the written permission of the author.
* * * * *

This book is a work of fiction. Places, events, and situations in this book are purely fictional and any resemblance to actual persons, living or dead, is coincidental
* * * * *

Formatting and cover design by Debora Lewis
deboraklewis@yahoo.com

Cover photo courtesy of Shutterstock

ISBN: 9798374703443

Acknowledgments

Writing fiction is an exercise in mental gymnastics to create a believable story that is accurate in detail but is also interesting to the vast world of readers who bring their personal histories into the mix. This intricate relationship between story line and reader is difficult to attain for a seasoned author but is a feat defying nature for a rookie.

My wife, Judy, provided invaluable support and perspective in this journey into an unknown world for me. My friends in our writing group provided continual support and assistance during this effort. Many thanks to authors Rich Wiley, Larry Tyree, Lorin Hicks, Vy Armour and Diana Ellis for their excellent assistance.

Finally, thank you to Debora Lewis of Warthog Publishing who brought this novel to the world.

ONE

During the autumn of 1780, the seeds of an organization created nearly a century later were planted. That organization, created to control financial and political power across international borders, remains in existence. Today, that organization, The Stony Point Directorate, has become synonymous with the words, "power, wealth, betrayal and treachery" and flourishes at the most exclusive addresses and dangerous, backwater alleys of the world."

On an early September morning, a lone rider cloaked in a gray cape over his dark blue uniform rode steadily on the road south to a farmhouse at Stony Point, New York and an appointment that would ever define the term treason. Traveling the road through lush forests and fertile farmlands of the Hudson River Valley, the man wanted to appear as unassuming as possible for fear of encountering British Army patrols scouring the area for traitors to the Crown and Colonial Army or militia patrols, lest they ask questions. The first frost of the season had not yet wrapped its icy fingers around the landscape, but he could feel the gnawing chill in his bones.

Several hours earlier, he had quietly ridden out through the gates of the Colonial Fort at West Point and expected to complete the twenty-one-mile journey to his meeting at the farmhouse before sunset.

The war was not going well, and some in the Colonial Officer Corps had become disenchanted with the entire affair. Feeling disrespected by his fellow patriots and believing the war was turning against the Colonials, General Benedict Arnold, Commander of the Fort at West Point, made a decision that would forever brand him as one of the most infamous people in what would become the United States of America. He made a conscious decision to abandon the Colonial Government loyalty oath he had signed in the presence of General George Washington at Valley Forge. On the evening of Thursday, September 21, 1780, and into the next morning, Arnold and British Major John Andre established their treacherous credentials at a house occupied by Attorney and Colonial spy Joshua Hett Smith. The two-story, white wood clapboard house, located atop a hill overlooking King's Ferry on the Hudson River south of Stony Point, New York became known forever as the "Treason House."

Two days later while riding back to the British lines, Major Andre was captured by three Colonial Militiamen. When the captors searched the British officer, they discovered the plans to West Point provided by Arnold. That encounter eventually became the genesis of a group guided by greed, power, and betrayal. Unlike the hapless Major Andre, Benedict Arnold escaped to London, joined the British Army, was given the rank of General and paid more than six thousand Pounds, currently valued at over 7 million U.S. Dollars. Major Andre, however, met his fate at the end of a colonial rope. That event sowed the seeds of a formidable group to be formed nearly a century later.

Benedict Arnold was revered as an American colonial hero until his personal interests overtook his patriotism and he concluded he would be better served assisting the wealthy and powerful British monarchy rather than helping the ungrateful, struggling Colonials. During his later years in England, while he enjoyed the fruits of his wealth, he was no hero to the British and in the new nation formed out of that struggle his name had become equivalent to the word "traitor."

TWO

On September 22, 1891, a century after General Arnold concluded that fateful meeting, five men of massive wealth and power and recognizing no formal international boundaries, met in one of the club rooms at their retreat compound on Wyndholm Island, Georgia and formed an association to benefit them no matter which way the winds of war or peace might blow. The date was not lost on them. In honor of the treacherous Stony Point meeting, one of the five founders, a great nephew of General Benedict Arnold, leaned back in his dark green leather armchair, took a sip of brandy from an exquisite crystal brandy snifter, and suggested the name, *The Stony Point Directorate*. From that day forward, they used governments, business and any other means and methods necessary to further their interests, observing no legal, ethical, or national boundaries. Thus, was the birth of this amoral assemblage.

Their motto, purloined from the famous statesman and patriot, Benjamin Franklin, who coined the phrase, *"Three can keep a secret if two are dead"* was not quite accurate for their purposes, although they were not hostile to its basic principle. The Directorate established an operational unit of individuals with skills and resources necessary for success and continued to build collective and personal empires on the back of civilization. That association matured into the current enterprise operating in the shadows of the modern world.

The furtive, exclusive group eventually became one of the most powerful confederations in the world. They established their headquarters on the property of one of the original five families just outside the major financial, business and power capital of the world at Long Island, New York.

THREE

1969 had been a somewhat unremarkable year for anyone engaged in the art of war. People lived and died. Property was destroyed and rebuilt, or not. Aircraft Commander, First Lieutenant Timothy L. Church looked at the green, rugged, mountainous landscape of the Republic of Viet Nam rapidly passing below the nose of his brown and forest green camouflaged vintage Douglas EC-47Q, twin engine propeller aircraft. It had come off the assembly line at the factory approximately a year before he had been born and proved to be more reliable than the leaders running this war. He and his crew had embarked on another mission to a fictional place in an airplane that did not exist doing something that was not happening, except it was very real, and so were the people and places.

Lieutenant Church and his co-pilot had similar backgrounds. Gray, dirty steel mills, foundries, oil refineries, chemical plants and railroad yards provided a bleak contrast to the vivid purple, green and red clouds occupying the sky. Blue was an alien hue seldom seen by the residents of the heavily industrialized cities and towns that coexisted within the coarse environment. An outsider would consider the environment as hostile as an alien planet, but the indigenous people only saw money. The lucky ones got out either through education or the military. Others through prison or death. The young aircraft commander knew he was one of the lucky ones. The military provided him with a modicum of financial security and a sense of worth not found working in a nineteenth century steel mill.

Tim Church seemed average in all outward aspects. Light brown hair, hazel eyes, medium height and weight complimented his affable nature. In his mind, achieving military rank was not the end goal. Surviving every day and keeping those in his charge safe were his primary objectives. He never considered himself to be overly intelligent, but that belied his 155 IQ that had been determined during his early Air Force testing days. He was not overly aggressive, but that, too, belied his nature to avoid conflict, but show no quarter when prompted to action. He just wanted to get along with most people and avoid the others. He could run when necessary, but respond with vicious, lethal intensity when cornered.

Suddenly, the hum of the engines was interrupted by the voice of the co-pilot, "Good morning, Peacock, this is Mace 72 heading 355, climbing to Base plus two-point-five."

"Good morning Mace 72, squawk 7224. You're cleared on course. Climb to your cruising altitude," the Controller replied in a neutral voice as if he were back home in central Illinois talking to his friend on the phone. The Aircraft Commander, also known as the Pilot, had been with this cockpit crew for the past several months.

"Well Boss, it looks like another day in paradise here in beautiful Southeast Asia, tiger hunting capitol of the world," declared the Co-Pilot, Second Lt. William R. ("Billy the Kid") Kidd. He must have had three breakfasts to be in such fine fettle this morning. Billy had survived four months "in country" and had not yet lost that enthusiastic exuberance associated with indestructible young pilots. According to his mother, Air Force pilots could never, ever walk on water because 'it always parts before they get there." A claim his mother never failed to mention to more than one of her cronies.

The Navigator interrupted their reverie with, "Turn to a heading of 345 degrees and hold level. I need to calibrate the equipment at the road intersection." Captain Ronald F. Johnson had been the Navigator on this crew for the past four months, and only had two weeks until his Date of Estimated Return from Overseas (DEROS). DEROS is that magic day when you return to the "World." The "World" for Captain Johnson was a family farm at the end of a dusty road somewhere in central Nebraska.

The road intersection was easy to locate. It was just northwest of the pristine white buildings that served as Regional Headquarters for an international tire and rubber company. A multi-national company that made its fortune from selling rubber products to large government and civilian markets that included both sides of this, and every other, conflict. The rubber tree groves and buildings were always in perfect, undamaged condition. The pilot imagined that was because no one ever tried to deface either the buildings or the rubber crop in the surrounding fields stretching for miles only minutes from his base. He always wondered how that company was fortunate enough to avoid friendly and enemy artillery, bombs or ground attacks that plagued the air base, several Army bases and especially the 76th Evacuation Hospital. The 76th Evac Hospital was a series of temporary metal buildings that housed the visible horrors of war inflicted upon the human body, as well as the invisible horrors of war residing in the minds of all concerned. No one left undamaged from that place.

The road intersection passed below the nose while Captain Johnson peered down through the "Driftmeter" installed through the belly of the airplane. It was much like a periscope with crosshairs. When the airplane passed over a known point, the Navigator calibrated his electronic navigation equipment from that known, exact spot on his map. The calibration was necessary to later identify precise enemy troop positions on the ground. The crew transmitted enemy location and communication information to others for intelligence and attack purposes. Sometimes, the information would even be used in "real time" to thwart an enemy ambush or attack.

"OK. We're good enough. Turn to 350 degrees and maintain until we either fall off the end of the earth, or I tell you to turn."

The venerable craft proceeded northward over lush green river valleys, and peaks sharp enough to slice through the skin of an airplane as if it were a ripe melon. A U.S. Air Force Air Traffic Control radio call broke the drone of the two Pratt & Whitney R-2000 propeller engines. "Mace 72, contact Panama on 322.6." That frequency change meant they had flown far enough north to come under air traffic control with "Panama Air Traffic Control Center" located near Da Nang AB. They would stay with this radar site for a while until making a left turn to go into the "Extreme Western DMZ."

The "Extreme Western DMZ" was code for Laos and Cambodia. Since the whole conflict was based on obfuscation by politicians and their funding sources, why should the names of places and other facts be any different. Moreover, our government insisted that we were not engaged in combat in Laos or Cambodia, only in Viet Nam. No one had a good explanation for how an airplane could take off from a runway in Laos loaded with bombs, rockets, or bullets, not leave Laotian airspace and return to its original location sans munitions. Of course, many of the aircraft had Royal Lao Air Force markings or no identifying markings but were flown by US military and civilian contractor crews in civilian clothing. The clandestine air force operated and funded by the United States Government did not exist. But that is another non-story.

"Mace 72, this is Panama, contact Invert on 334.5. See you later."

Billy the Kid replied, "Thanks. Going 334.5".

The flightpath now turned left to leave South Viet Nam airspace and into Laos to an area that was home to a series of trails and roads called the "Ho Chi Minh Trail." Their route through the "Extreme Western DMZ" took the aircraft a few miles north of Tchepone, Laos, the base for various 23mm, 57mm, 75mm and 100mm anti-aircraft guns as well as SA-2 surface-to-air missiles that could shoot down an airplane at 100,000 feet above the ground. Since this EC-47Q flew below 10,000 feet, each of these weapons posed a threat.

The aircraft passed over landscape that became more verdant and severe with sharper peaks and deeper valleys while the crew worked at their stations using flak vests as seat cushions. The vests were not really that cushy, but they did give a layer of assumed protection from various projectiles coming up from the ground. The vests may or may not stop a weak bullet or piece of shrapnel, but that was better than nothing.

The day was clear and bright. Droning engines provided a mesmerizing hum while the crew and their aircraft cruised lazily north along the "Ho Chi Minh Trail" toward the target area at the Mu Ghia Pass, the main artery for men and supplies moving south out of North Viet Nam to the end users in Cambodia, Laos and South Viet Nam.

Flying an unarmed aircraft at a blistering, ninety-five miles per hour only a few thousand feet above or below mountain peaks had become routine and almost mind numbing. The mission tasked them to locate the enemy who tried to hide from the searching eyes and ears of the aircrew. When discovered, enemy location and troop strength information was passed to other aircraft or ground troops who would try to remodel those facilities with rockets, bomb or bullets. The mouse tried to hide from the cat, but when the enemy believed they had been discovered, they tried to "kill the messenger."

That day, the crew successfully located large enemy troop and equipment concentrations while causing them to believe the crew had missed the targets. Then things changed abruptly. Maybe some guy on the ground got bored or was having a bad day and failed to get the memo about not confronting the aircraft to arouse a deadly response. Whatever the reason, the guy, or girl, was good or lucky enough to add some extra lead to the left engine.

The first clue that the situation had changed was the sounds of metal thudding into metal. Those clues were immediately followed by loud banging accompanied by the sound of explosions, and a severe yaw to the left that scared the hell out the entire crew. The left engine shook, sputtered, coughed, banged and threw long licks of flame. The airplane abruptly lost altitude and gained airspeed. The cockpit crew shut down the engine to stop the fire, explosions, and the potential for the left wing to separate from the rest of the aircraft resulting in an asymmetrical flight condition, and loss of lift. The loud sounds and flames ceased, but the airplane continued its descending left turn.

Single engine operation could not keep this heavily laden aircraft airborne in level flight. The crew of eight, comprised of two pilots, a navigator, a flight mechanic and four men in back with their specialized electronic equipment not intended for use by anyone other than the crew, readied themselves for a crash. They prepared to destroy classified documents, equipment and even the aircraft to deny the enemy.

"Mayday! Mayday! Mayday! Mace 72 is declaring an emergency. Left Engine out. Cannot maintain altitude. Request clearance present position direct Nakon Phanom." The pilot had made the emergency call with the measured speech of someone reciting from memory. No panic or alarm, only a controlled cadence resulting from hours of training and experience.

"This is Invert. Mace 72. state your fuel status, number of souls on-board and your intentions."

"We have one thousand pounds of fuel and eight souls on board. Our Altitude is Base plus 6. We cannot maintain level flight but have a controlled descent and request present position direct NKP."

"Roger Mace 72. You are cleared present position direct to the Nakon Phanom airport."

Suddenly, a new voice joined the conversation. Two World War II propeller driven vintage attack aircraft used by the Air Force for aircrew Search and Rescue operations and ground attack had heard the radio transmissions and flew to assist the crew if the aircraft crashed. "Invert. This is Sandy 21 & 22. We are available to assist."

"Roger, Sandy 21. This is Invert. You are cleared to join Mace 72. Vector is 290 degrees for fifteen miles. Mace 72 is at Base plus 5."

Billy the Kid called Johnson on the interphone, "Nav. Injuries and damage report."

The Navigator replied. "No injuries. Some holes in the left side and floor. No real damage except for a hole in one seat, seat cushion and flak vest."

"Roger Nav" What the hell is the deal with the…?"

The Navigator somberly replied, "A round came through the bottom of my seat while I was standing. Will never ride seated again. Always stay standing"

"Mace 72 this is Sandy 21. We have you in sight and are coming up on your six. 22 will make a visual."

"Roger Sandy."

Mace 72 this is Sandy 22. You have some holes in the left wing and belly. Some oil streaming from Number One. The rest is OK."

"Thanks Sandy. If you guys would like to come along, we would certainly appreciate it. We can't maintain level flight but should be able to make NKP since the terrain is sloping down as we get closer to the airport."

"Roger Mace 72. We don't have anything better to do for a while. We'll take you home."

The karsts and deep valleys passing below the crippled airplane resembled the hills of West Virginia where you go from straight up to straight down. Dark green vegetation slowly morphed to red clay then to brown dirt as the wounded aircraft moved farther away from the mountains to the Mekong River valley. Fifty nautical miles of controlled descent offered a surreal collage of trees, bushes, thatched roofs and life in a place with more than its share of people with guns, rockets and stick launchers. Yes, "Stick Launchers." Occasionally, low flying helicopters were damaged and crashed when long sticks were shot into the air from crude, but efficient, slingshots and became entangled in the rotor blades.

"Mace 72, this is Invert. "A Jolly Green has launched from NKP to join the parade. Estimate its intercept in about ten minutes." That was a comforting message. NKP Rescue had sent a large Air Force rescue helicopter with dedicated, highly trained crewmen known by the call sign, "Jolly Green" to locate and transport to a friendly location.

The presence of the two A-1H "Skyraiders", probably influenced the Pathet Lao to stay hidden. A good decision since the A-1H carried machine guns, rockets, bombs and anything else the armor guys could hang on the airplane.

The eerily quiet drone of the remaining engine was interrupted when the radio came to life, "Mace 72 this is Invert. Contact NKP Tower on 255.7. They're expecting you."

"Mace 72, roger."

Billy the Kid changed radio frequencies, squeezed the mic button and said, "NKP Tower this is Mace 72 declaring an emergency and requesting an immediate landing. We are at two thousand feet, maintaining a controlled descent and have the field in sight. This will be a one-time attempt since we cannot climb on one engine or make a second try."

"Mace 72, NKP Tower, you are cleared to land runway one-five, altimeter 28.83, winds 070 degrees at 17 gust 30, emergency equipment in place."

"Tower, this Sandy 21. Cap is crossing the river. We are returning to station. Good Luck, Mace."

"Thanks Sandy. Buy you guys a beer when we can."

The pilot thought, *Terrific. The maximum allowable crosswind for the C-47, is twenty-five knots, and that is with both engines and no problems. This beat-up old bird already wants to turn left due to excessive thrust from the engine on the right side. So, with less lift and increased drag, this heavily laden airplane simply does not want to fly. The best plan would be to land between wind gusts.*

The approach flight path crossed the river from the east with a left turn onto a long, straight final approach. The Mekong separated Nakon Phanom, Thailand from Thakhek, Laos, and the US did not control Thakhek. The joke was, "It only cost one Baht to go east across the river to Thakhek, but a million Baht to come back." Not that funny.

The east wind wanted to push the airplane to the right side of the runway, so the cock-eyed angle of the airplane pointing to the left was helpful. Strong gusts, however, kept battering the damaged war bird making level flight difficult. They crossed the river at a respectable 700 feet, noticing that the occupants on several boats were keenly aware of their plight, reminding the pilot of hungry jackals watching an injured prey. Only one chance to make a landing on the runway. As the aircraft approached the end of the runway at one hundred feet above the threshold while aligned to the left of centerline, a heavy gust lifted the left wing, and pushed the airplane towards the right side of the runway. Engine power on the right side was a good thing since that gave the craft a tendency to turn left pushing the craft back to the runway centerline. Almost as soon as the wing lifted, the craft sank when the gust died. Just above the runway, the right throttle was pulled back to idle, the airplane dropped quickly to the tarmac and rolled to a stop on the right edge of the pavement.

Billy the Kid activated the emergency evacuation alarm bell, and everyone ran for the single exit door at the left, rear side of the fuselage to get a safe distance from the damaged craft.

That was it. The crew made it. The airplane made it. The "special equipment" made it. Secrets remained secret.

The Crash Rescue guys came to the airplane and confirmed all crew was off the craft with no fire threat.

A tug came out and dragged Mace 72 from the runway. After the damaged piece of Government equipment was moved to a maintenance area for inspection and repairs, the crew retrieved all the classified and personal equipment, including the poor flak vest that did not protect the top of the fuselage where a hole was prominently displayed. It was a nice, round hole, and the bullet most likely suffered little or no damage. That vest eventually found its way to a place of honor hanging on the wall in Squadron Operations.

Everyone knows the job isn't finished until the paperwork is complete. While the aircraft commander completed maintenance forms, the Chief of Maintenance came up to him and said, "Nice job, Lieutenant, and Merry Christmas!" During this entire event, they had forgotten that it was Christmas Eve. Off to the Intelligence Section for the mission debriefing.

That night, maintenance crews changed the engine and repaired the holes. The EC-47Q and its crew had a mission to fly the next morning. They were scheduled to fly back to that "magical" place that didn't exist to the north and east of Nakon Phanom, in an airplane that didn't exist carrying a crew with no identities. That description put it all in the same category as Santa and his Elves at his North Pole Toy Shop. The only problem was that all of it was real except to the people who did not want to admit the aircrew was expendable.

The Lieutenant had just had his first real encounter with armor that failed to defeat the threat. But to quote an infamous saying, "Nothing is too good for the Troops, and that is exactly what they'll get." A strange feeling of betrayal began to creep into the consciousness of at least two members of the crew that didn't exist. It expressed the inadequate body armor and the knowledge that if the airplane had gone down, Search and Rescue would attempt to retrieve the crew, and ensure the aircraft and equipment were destroyed beyond recognition. If they could not retrieve the people, then those people would cease to exist in the eyes of the government. The crew never really believed the part about our government leaders never abandoning the people, or did they? Assignment to a "Spook Squadron" was an assignment to deceit, fabrication, and intentional inaccuracies.

Meanwhile, in the warm sun and gentle breezes of the Central Highlands, the tea and rubber plantations continued to prosper, and the supply of very lucrative war materiel continued to flow to both sides at maximum levels. Someone somewhere was making a lot of money from those protected profit centers.

Eventually, the pilots would receive medals for returning the crew, the aircraft and the secrets to safety. But the date, time and place in the narrative known as the "Citation to accompany the Award" would have no relationship to any real event.

This was his first, but by no means his last encounter with the ubiquitous doctrines known as "Betrayal" and "Plausible Deniability." The young officer had no idea how intimately he would become involved or when it would happen, but he was certain it would happen again.

FOUR

The worn, weary man gazed into the gradual onset of a late January dusk from his window in the "White House." The weak sun radiated pale orange shafts of light out from under a heavy gray layer of snow-laden clouds. The buildings and trappings of Pennsylvania Avenue representing the greatest power in the world gave mixed signals to his tired consciousness. He justified many decisions with the old excuse, "the greatest good for the greatest number", but long ago he had decided it would not be a good idea to use that defense when Saint Peter started asking questions.

In the waning light and omnipresent solitude, he walked to his desk and picked up the secure telephone. He was about to do it again. He was about to betray a group of men, their families, himself, and his country. The citizens of his nation had always believed that we never intentionally left anyone behind, but he knew that was not always the case. He quietly said, "Execute Operation Arnold." His statement was acknowledged by a serious female voice, "Yes, sir, execute Operation Arnold. The time is nineteen-thirty-one hours." He placed the black telephone handset in its cradle, looked down at his desk and paused for just an instant. Someone had decided to call the plan, "Operation Arnold" in recognition of Benedict Arnold the famous Colonial Officer who betrayed his country. How very apropos for a member of the Stony Point Directorate. One of his ancestors had been a founding member, but he never thought he would find himself on such a personal level directly condemning men to their ultimate fate. That was always left to others in some distant place, but not this time. No "Plausible Deniability" this time.

On the other side of the world in a god-forsaken place, men would be left behind. They would not be claimed by their country. They were expendable, and he knew it.

In an ornate room at a foreign capital, a high-ranking official of his government seated with many others at an exquisitely polished mahogany table would lie to the world, and other men would pay the price. He would quietly utter lies and misrepresentations all allegedly for the good of the country, but very good for the "Directorate" as it was known by its members

The long national nightmare of the war in Southeast Asia was coming to an end, and soon the healing process would begin. For some it would never end. Some would never allow it to end. But time would work its magic, and eventually the episode would slowly become lost in the mist of history. But for those who knew the reality of the situation it would always represent a "betrayal" of those who were sacrificed for "the good of the many" and there was more than one man still alive to keep the secret.

FIVE

Early April brought cool breezes slipping between buildings forming the canyon known as the 300 block of South Dearborn Street, Chicago, Illinois. The appointed place had limited parking, and Special Agent Timothy Church refused to pay for a parking lot. In short order, he would receive his assigned parking spot in the Federal Parking Garage on the west side of the 400 block of South Federal Street. But until that happened, he was relegated to the law enforcement visitor's parking area consisting of the streets around the Federal complex. Law enforcement parked on any of the side streets at no cost if the police radio microphone hung by its spiral cord over the rear-view mirror, the signal for the local Chicago PD beat officer to write two tickets per vehicle at the same time. Why, *"Two at the same time?"* you might ask. Because of a great working relationship. The City Attorney dismissed all the citations, but the beat cop made his ticket quota for the day twice as fast than if he ticketed civilian cars one at a time.

Welcome to daily life in the "Second City", "Hog Butcher to the world" and home to the perennial losers, the Chicago Cubs. *Pardon me,* he chuckled to himself. He had been a White Sox fan ever since he could remember.

This was his first professional return to Chicago since leaving the police department nine years ago, and he was looking forward to working in the Loop. Walking north on Dearborn Street brought back the sights, sounds, and smells of the city. The pale, distant, sometimes surly, solemn pedestrians who never looked at anyone. The cacophony of trucks, busses, taxis, limos, and cars all fighting to get somewhere, anywhere. The sweet aroma of the donut shop with its coffee and treats at the corner of Jackson and Dearborn. The pungent aromas of diesel engines and street people. The distant metallic rumble of the grimy elevated trains passing over their antiquated steel bridges a block to the south. The ubiquitous accumulated trash wet with a late season melting snow caressing the curbs and sewer grates.

He was a little early for his appointment to meet the Special-Agent-in-Charge at his new digs. After squeezing his unmarked federal police sedan into a parking place on South Dearborn Street, he stepped into the Dunkin Donut shop. The coffee was much better than at the Federal Building cafeteria, and a chair at the window provided a great view of the entrances to the various buildings.

After consuming a chocolate covered donut, and a black coffee, he crossed Jackson Street and entered the Dirksen Federal Building. This was the headquarters of the United States Department of the Treasury, Bureau of Alcohol, Tobacco and Firearms, Chicago District Office, lovingly known by the good and the bad as ATF, former employer of Elliot Ness, the famous "Untouchable." Tim had not been in that building for several years, but it looked the same. It always looked the same. He was reporting for duty at his new office. Agents usually avoided an assignment to New York,

Chicago or Los Angeles like the plague, but he grew up in the area, and liked the place. There was always something to do, like shovel snow and wear extra clothes in the winter or sweat gallons in the summer heat and humidity.

Time had come to meet the new boss. Mary Anne, the office receptionist sent him back to Alice, secretary to the boss. He introduced himself and handed her an envelope with his transfer paperwork. "Welcome to Chicago, Mister Church. Have a seat. Mr. Trojanowski will be with you in a minute"

Daniel Z. Trojanowski and Tim had first met during his initial job interview. Tim was a city police officer when he applied to several federal law enforcement agencies, and ATF was the first agency to interview and accept him.

The boss was sitting behind his desk looking out onto Jackson Street, totally engrossed in a staring contest with an indignant pigeon perched on the orange, metal Calder sculpture across the street. Tim announced his presence with a hearty, "Good Morning, Sir."

"Yeah. The same to you," the Boss growled.

"Dan, Sir, I know you're a busy man, but I need to ask if you've pulled any fire alarms lately?"

"No!" he fired back. "Now, I just sit here and make the big bucks, Asshole!"

You may be wondering what this "fire alarm" business is all about. The phrase is not a code for any clandestine operation to destroy a nefarious plot by some Mafia gang, terrorist cell or international illegal arms cartel. It goes back to when Dan was a street Agent serving an arrest warrant on a young Appalachian man who had sold stolen pistols and shotguns in a "Sting" operation. Dan, Tim and several other law enforcement officers went to the house in the Detroit suburb River Rouge, listed as the last known address for the suspect. When Dan knocked on the front door, a scrawny girl in her late teens wearing a tee shirt and old levis opened the door and asked in a distinct Appalachian drawl, "What do you guys want?"

Dan, in his authoritative voice said, "I am Special Agent Trojanowski, with United States Department of the Treasury, Bureau of Alcohol, Tobacco and Firearms, and we have an arrest warrant for Billy Joe Tiner for violations of the Federal Firearms Laws."

The girl responded with, "That's my brother, but he ain't here. Fire Alarms! Fire Alarms! He ain't never pulled no damn fire alarms!"

A bit stunned, Dan replied, "Firearms, like guns."

The girl came back with, "Oh yeah, he does guns, but he ain't never pulled no damn fire alarms."

Those were much simpler days.

The men talked about the "Good Old Days" and the life up to the current time for a while, when Tim learned his friend was fascinated by a shabbily dressed street hustler working Jackson Street at the entrance to the Monadnock Building. The boss described how he watched the "panhandler" start the day at his spot somewhere around 7:30 AM, and hustle until about 1:00 PM when he would walk south on Federal towards Van Buren Street and a city parking lot. Dan recounted, "I watched as the "Poor Soul" looked around to make certain that no one was watching, then pulled out a wad of cash about the size of a softball. One day, I followed the guy at the end of his 'shift' and watched as he pulled out of a parking garage in his new Jaguar. I nearly decided to retire and take over the street corner location on Jackson but thought it might be too much work."

"Since you like the city you're assigned to Group One, here at the District Office. Your area is everything within the city limits. Group Two has the northern counties and Group Three has the southern counties. The Eisenhower Expressway divides the north and south. Time to meet your Group Supervisor, Kelly Marshall. Ten years on the job here in Chicago, former Reno cop." They walked to the Group One office at the other end of the building. He met the Group Supervisor, took the only available desk, and resumed his career in Chicago.

"Tim, your file shows you are in the Air Force Reserve at O'Hare. Is that right?"

"Yes, I have a few years to go before I can retire."

"What do you do in the Reserve?"

"I work as an Intelligence Officer. The Federal Government is a military–friendly employer that allows me to finish my twenty years for a military retirement. I also like Intelligence because it provided a break from the streets and keeps me in the information loop regarding various nasty governments and groups throughout the world."

SIX

Several seasons had passed in the "Second City." Tim had settled into a routine providing enough excitement for someone of his age, but he still dealt with the nameless, faceless group of people in the shadows and alleys of America and the world.

On a typical November day, Tim stepped out of the Federal Building into the world of tall skyscrapers smothered and covered by clouds coming off the cold waters of Lake Michigan. The scene should have sounded warning alarms in his head and gut. People on the streets were hunched over trying to protect themselves from the stinging pellets of sleet racing down from the clouds to attack the grimy streets and sidewalks and anything else that might be encountered. Without warning, a voice from behind called his name. "Hey Tim!" "Hey Tim!" He turned to find an old friend from many years ago.

"Hey Tim. Ron Johnson. Remember me from about twenty years ago in a land far away?" Tim took a second to confirm it was his Navigator from the Christmas Eve mission over the Extreme Western DMZ.

"Ron, you look a bit older, but I recognize the "lost look" in your eyes. How have you been? What are you doing in Chicago?"

"I happened to be in the neighborhood and thought we might get together for a bit."

"Ron, what have you been doing since you left Pleiku in the beautiful Republic of Viet Nam?"

The man shrugged and weakly smiled, "I do some contract work for international companies. You have a few minutes to talk?"

For some reason, his request came across as more than an old friend asking whether Tim had time for coffee and war stories. There was something in his manner and demeanor, that said Tim should comply. It was an uneasy, albeit very intriguing feeling. He agreed, and they walked toward the Dunkin Donut coffee shop in silence. As they approached the entrance Ron continued walking past the doorway and turned right down a narrow, grimy street. He did not slow until they came to the entrance of a tired, old building on Plymouth Court. He opened the door and motioned to go inside.

Once inside he said, "I have a quiet place we can talk without any disturbances."

The elevator opened at the third floor directly across the hallway from a door with a brass plate identifying the offices of the "United States Imagery and Mapping Agency." Tim did not recognize the US Government agency.

Not knowing whether to be worried, angry or happy, he said, "Ron, what in the world is going on here?"

Ron calmly replied, "You are about to enter a world of great possibilities." He opened the door to an ante-room devoid of any furniture or wall hangings. Only strategically placed cameras were visible along the crown molding where the beige walls met the ceiling. Before Ron touched the door handle to the stark chamber, the electronic lock quietly clicked. The entrance opened to a narrow corridor with a door only a few feet away on the right and another non-descript door about half-way down the brightly lighted hallway on the left. They stopped in front of the first door and waited until they heard another metallic door lock disengage. Ron turned the handle, and ushered Tim into the room. It was a very efficient room. A lone gray steel US Government chair was on one side of a small, rectangular gray metal table that appeared to have been used by Patton in Europe. The walls were a dull, pale green and tan matching the mood and the furniture. Harsh neon ceiling light fixtures completed the sterile landscape. Although not readily visible, Tim sensed several pinhole surveillance cameras and microphones secreted around the room that reminded him of many similar rooms he had experienced in his military intelligence and civilian law enforcement career. This time, he had the distinct feeling of complete vulnerability. He had not chosen the room, the chair, or his position in the room. He felt at a complete disadvantage. Very disconcerting. His chair was placed so he could not see the entry door behind him.

"Sorry for the cloak and dagger, but it really is necessary."

Seconds later the door opened behind Tim and a voice said, "Welcome Tim. Thank you for coming on such short notice. Ron will provide more information."

After a short, inaudible exchange of words with Ron, the voice left the room and the door clicked closed. The voice had remained behind Tim. He never turned around to see the source, but it had the sound and tone of someone more accustomed to giving orders than receiving them.

Ron sat in the chair across from Tim and began to speak in a weary monotone. "You will be contacted by your new employer with personnel, financial and other information. But before I go, I have something you should read. You will not be able to keep the document nor reveal its contents to anyone without explicit authorization. Do you understand?"

Tim quietly said, "Yes."

Ron began, "After we left Pleiku, the squadron moved to Ubon Airfield, Thailand and changed its unit call sign from 'Mace' to 'Eagle.' As the Paris Peace Accords were being signed, a crew was flying a reconnaissance mission to verify certain North Vietnamese and Viet Cong military activities. Of course, our government was not supposed to be flying those missions."

Ron removed a folded document from his coat pocket and placed it on the table. "Read this." It was several pieces of plain typing paper. No letterhead or any other identifying marks.

Tim took the pages and began to read. His eyes focused on the text as he began to learn the story of an aircraft and its crew.

One night, just before midnight an aircraft with the call sign, "Eagle 25", departed Ubon Airfield, Thailand on a night intelligence gathering mission to monitor enemy traffic flowing down the Ho Chi Minh Trail. Such movement of men and material by the communists would constitute a direct violation of the Paris Peace Accords on their part. At 0125 hours Eagle 25 was flying along the Ho Chi Minh Trail and reported to controllers on the ground that they were observing ground fire directed toward them from the jungle covered mountains in Laos. The last message received came five to ten minutes later when they reported that everything was all right. When the aircraft failed to return to friendly control, the crew was declared missing.

Two days later, based on their last known position, a search and rescue mission found the aircraft had impacted the ground in the forested mountains of Laos. A search team was dispatched to examine the wreckage. Three rescue specialists and an intelligence expert were on the ground for over forty minutes to complete their survey. They found three burned bodies still strapped in their seats in the cockpit. They also found partial remains of another officer outside the wreckage. Four days later the remains were identified.

They did not recover the remains of the four enlisted crewmembers from the back of the airplane. Sources said there was evidence that the four sergeants bailed out of the aircraft and survived. They supported that theory in several ways.

First. No remains, or any other evidence that they died in the crash, were found.

Second. The search team could not find the men. Their seatbelts had been unbuckled, and their parachutes, along with their sensitive equipment, were gone. This indicated to the Search and Rescue personnel that all four men had time to follow standard operating procedures and jettisoned all the sensitive electronics gear prior to bailing out themselves.

Third. The jump door was kicked away and could not be found at or near the crash site.

Fourth. North Vietnamese Army units operating in this immediate area had radio communications to their higher headquarters monitored by US intelligence personnel. Seven hours after last contact with Eagle 25, the first of several intercepted messages discussing the capture of four flyers was received. These intercepts continued for three months. Those messages remain classified today.

Fifth. A Laotian road watcher for the US reported observing these same captives being moved along a road in Laos. This sighting corroborated the information from the intercepts.

Sixth. This information, along with post-capture photographs of the four sergeants, was provided to the US Ambassador to Laos during one of his daily morning briefings. Continued intercept information revealed communist personnel interrogated them on several occasions as they were moved along a clear line through Laos, to Hanoi, then airlifted to Moscow.

Seventeen days after the aircraft was lost, all seven men were declared Killed in Action under a Presumed Finding of Death in spite of the fact that our government knew differently.

Five years later, the mother of one of the sergeants heard columnist Jack Anderson, on "Good Morning America", describe a Pathet Lao radio communiqué that described the capture of four "air pirates" on the same day as the airplane carrying her son was shot down. Records indicated it was the only aircraft downed during that time frame.

Tim folded the paper, lowered his eyes, and studied the floor as his anger and years of frustration with the "system" pushed up from the depths of the place he thought they had been buried. The government knew four of its airmen were under duress in the custody of hostile foreign governments. Those men remained alive for an unknown time after their capture. Their government had abandoned them for political purposes. What were these people that made these decisions?

Were they human? What about the code of honor, ethics, humanity these people espoused in their very public profiles? The crewmen were expendable in this little political game. The "Chicken Hawk" politicians controlled by ego, money and power had abandoned these men. The same people who had been too busy with their private business and personal and political lives to put themselves on the line for another. How many of them had "bone spurs" or "flat feet" when they were called to serve others? They probably had business or political interests in Southeast Asian rubber plantations. Another act of betrayal.

Without speaking, Tim handed the document to Ron who returned it to his coat pocket. Silently, they walked out of the room. When they got to the street, Tim looked at Ron. Each gave a slight nod, turned, and walked in opposite directions. Tim wanted to do something. Something to make them pay. But who was "Them?" He slowly crossed the street back to his office with one word etched into his psyche. "Betrayal."

SEVEN

The new year had begun much the same as previous years. The local Chicago nightly news droned on about the number of local deaths and injuries sustained as the result of gunfire, the horrors of wars and civil unrest in the world and the financial news. He turned off the television, and the room descended into an uneasy sleep. Something was calling Tim from an unfathomable area of his tired brain. Was it an alter ego developed in his beleaguered past? Whatever it was, it just kept nagging at the solitude.

He had been on the job with ATF much too long and he planned to spend a few more years in the quagmire of federal law enforcement where no one wanted a Special Agent to be too "special" and get the job done. Make cases, but only those that were acceptable to the political powers. Success outside of those rules brought sniping from Congress, powerful political support groups and those wanting to maintain the status quo, i.e. their jobs, their power, their wealth. That was the mood when the phone rang just after midnight. He was not the "Duty Agent." No one with any sense would call him at this hour. He lifted the receiver and said nothing. After a few seconds, the voice said, "Tim? Are you there? It's Ron."

Why was he calling at this hour? Maybe he was in Hawaii and forgot the time zone changes. Tim hesitated, more out of confusion than consternation. Finally, he said, "Ron, because once upon a time you were an official Air Force navigator, I believe you know how to read a watch. Why are you calling at this ungodly hour?" Tim also wondered why he hadn't heard from Ron for over a year.

Ron flatly countered, "Tim, your pay is based on a twenty-four-hour day. Besides, I have some news you might want to hear. Remember when we talked a few months ago? Well, your resume is requested. Do not use a government form. Prepare it the same as any business resume on plain white paper and send it to the address we mailed to your Post Office box."

Surprised at the reference to his Post Office Box, he asked, "How do you know I have a Post Office box?"

"Good question. You have a week to get the resume to the address. The phone number I included with the address can be used to verify receipt of the document and is your primary contact point. The recipient is seeking people with a military, law enforcement, firearms, explosives and intelligence background."

"Then what?"

"You'll be contacted. I need to run, it's late." The phone went dead.

Two days later, Tim mailed the resume to a Post Office box in rural Virginia.

EIGHT

Months dragged by. Mundane chores like buying a dozen stolen automatic weapons from a brain damaged burglar, collecting, transporting and destroying three explosive devices and arresting a sleazy bar owner intent on collecting the insurance proceeds from an arson fire at his dive kept the senior agent busy.

Later, when he tried to remember the timeline of his life after Chicago, Tim remembered the day in question had dawned with a painfully bright sun moving through an unsullied, magnificently azure sky. It was during this moment of unplanned euphoria that curiosity overwhelmed Tim. He called the phone number Ron had provided for this alleged new job.

After two rings, a flat, female voice said, "Hello." That was it. Just a nearly metallic voice. He waited, but no further response came through the phone.

He said, "Is this 800-999-0001?"

Several uncomfortable seconds elapsed with no response. Using his best professional, courteous, compassionate voice he asked, "I'm calling to see if you received my resume."

"Yes. You will be contacted at the appropriate time." Click, the line went quiet.

That was it. His suspicions were confirmed. This was something that did not exist. Hell, the voice may well have been a man using some type of masking device. The voice seemed to know who was calling, even though he had used a Government Centrex System telephone that provides no caller information.

Maybe Ron Johnson would call him, but probably not. This had been a one-way street since that first mysterious meeting in that non-descript room. Besides, when Tim returned to that building on Plymouth Court the next day, the building directory did not list a US Government office anywhere in the building. When he went to the third floor and looked out as the elevator doors opened, there was no official sign on the door or wall. The offices of the National Imagery and Mapping Agency (NIMA) no longer existed at that location. Standing in the hallway staring at the blank wall and door, he noticed a young woman coming toward the elevator. She glanced in his direction much like a baby rabbit looks at a coyote.

Hoping to defuse a tense situation, Tim displayed the gold ATF Special Agent badge. "Excuse me. I am trying to locate the offices of the United States National Imagery and Mapping Agency. I was told they are here on the third floor."

The woman looked at him and the badge, relaxed a bit and said, "No one with that name is here. That space has been vacant for nearly a year. Sorry."

"Thanks." He knew something was a little out of the ordinary, but so was his past with Ron Johnson, et. al. He knew this had been another incident that "never happened."

It all fit. This was nothing, and now he was involved with it. The story of his career. Confusion. Obfuscation. Nothing clear or normal.

The short walk back to the office was a blur of sights, sounds, smells and racing thoughts. He knew something significant had happened, and now he would wait for the next "shoe to drop" in the bewildering mosaic of his life. Bad guys, administrative geeks and self-centered politicians awaited his return to this current life, or so he thought.

NINE

The sun was high over the Loop and downtown Chicago was buzzing with lunch hour turmoil. People and traffic were everywhere, moving in all directions. Tim looked down on the scene from his office and thought how it reminded him of watching an ant farm. The office intercom line buzzed. When he answered, the receptionist said, "Mr. Church, you have a visitor. A Lt. Don Smulski with Chicago PD."

He did not know a Lt Don Smulski with the Chicago Police, but never professed to know everyone or everything.

"Thanks. Send him back."

Tim was closing his computer screen when the policeman came through the office door.

"Hi Tim. It's me Don Smulski!"

"The hell you are!"

This was crazy. He had been in some obtuse situations where the reality of the moment did not coincide with the reality of reality. But then, those persons, places and things never existed, anyway. In seconds, his mind went through too may scenarios with too many questions to result in any plausible answers other than this should not be happening.

"Tim, would you care to go for a little walk to get some coffee? Would you do that for the Chicago Police Department?"

They left the building, and walked toward Daley Plaza, a place with coffee vendors, benches, people, and background noise. A quiet walk for two old comrades. The walk must have taken ten minutes, but for Tim time seemed to freeze, and race, at the same time. They ordered two black coffees from a vendor cart and found a recently vacated concrete bench. After a few seconds, the sounds of the crowded city attacked the senses. Taxis, trucks and busses contributed to the harsh, discordant mixture of sounds intertwined with a cornucopia of colors cascading the senses from the human interlopers all splashed across a pallet of grays and browns of the city. This was a perfect place to have a private conversation. Just enough noise to cover normal speech frequencies, but quiet enough to have a muted chat concealed from prying snoops. Two middle-aged men in inexpensive business suits perfectly blended into the confusion of the city.

The silence was broken when Tim asked, "Well, Ron did you get married, change your name and join CPD?"

"If you check, Lt. Smulski is only a few years younger than us, and has been on medical leave from CPD since last Christmas when he fell while climbing a ladder to collect evidence. He is currently visiting his sister in Australia, and I only needed his name for a few minutes at your office. I am positive that the man will never know he has been the victim of identity theft for fifteen minutes."

"Ron, why all this? You disappeared from the planet immediately after we met the last time. But I must admit that I never really looked for you. It was all too strange. Just like this is all too strange."

"Remember that resume you sent to Virginia? We want to know if you are still interested. Some administrative and operational changes were required, and the position remains with a private organization involved in many things on the international stage. This group has been in existence for many decades and participates in many arenas. Unlike the Government, this group can afford to pay you a more lucrative salary and benefits package. You will still use your management, surveillance, weapons and explosives skills and your knowledge of military, law enforcement and intelligence procedures."

"Sounds like a civilian version of the CIA.'

"Some people might share that view, but not all. When you made the phone call, your timing was impeccable. We recently had a new opening, and you are next in line for the job offer."

Tim looked around and smiled ruefully, "So what happened to my assumed predecessor? Is he still alive and not currently either incarcerated or lounging in some off-the-grid medical facility?"

Ron sipped his coffee as he watched two young office workers stroll past.

"Ron why am I in the middle of a public square, drinking coffee with an old Air Force buddy from a time and a place that never existed, and talking about things that I should not know? And what does that mean to an old ATF Agent like me? Once again. Why are we here?"

"The answer is quite simple. You fit the job description. As I said, your resume was filed, not destroyed. Your background, our background, contain a unique set of assets deemed desirable for specific projects. You have never been off our radar."

"Why are you telling me all this? I still work for ATF, and I certainly am not leaving the job when retirement is so close."

"We know. You might consider this as the "Perfect Storm" of circumstances. You are eligible to retire, you have no civilian job lined up and your resume is still on file. You really are the right man at the right time and place for the job."

"And if I decline the job offer, will I be lost at sea or fall from a cliff? Or will I be like the guys from Eagle 25?"

"Real life is not that dramatic. Personnel screw-ups, Inspection Division investigations or any number of problems can get in the way of retirement and pensions. You know how incompetent the Government can be. But we go back a long way and I have no reason to screw you. This is a real opportunity to do good work while getting excellent pay and benefits. Money that can be placed anywhere in the world. It happens every day. It's just not broadcast to the public. They think those things only happen on TV or in books. We both know the truth about that."

"Let's pretend I take the position. How would that happen?"

"Well, you have fifty-seven days to your retirement eligibility date. You have accrued sixty days of Annual Leave, and one year accrued Sick Leave. You could walk out the door today. We will pay a "signing bonus" in excess of the funds you would receive if you waited and start on our payroll the next day. Your new housing will be arranged at a location and quality to which you would like to become accustomed. The small details can be negotiated. Your salary and benefits will start at twenty grand per month with a liberal expense account. What do you think?"

"What would I actually do?"

"You would supervise and conduct investigative activities similar to those you currently perform. You would detect and deter any Intellectual Property losses, assist with R&D, manage assets, create and control operational plans, and perform any other duties required to protect these systems, but in a private capacity. A unique position."

"You mean I won't exist again, doing things that don't happen."

"Yes, but at a better pay scale that is very real."

Tim stared up into the cloudless cobalt sky. American Airlines was in a climbing turn to avoid disturbing downtown Chicago. When the sun flashed off the fuselage like a bright laser, Tim considered it a sign that this was a deal he could not refuse.

"OK. I'll take the job. Now what?"

"Good. Just go back to work, send your retirement request up the chain and wait for a call. The call will come before you get your papers to personnel."

The sun was still shining, and a warm zephyr coursed sleepily between the tall buildings creating a pleasant sensation with the hum of city traffic. Ron stood up and blended into the sights and sounds of Chicago. Gone in seconds. Tim sat there trying to bring some semblance of calm back to the inner recesses of his brain that had been dormant for so many years. A small voice probed his psyche, "What have you done?" He started walking back to the office to complete the paperwork that would release him to the vagaries of the rest of his life. As he crossed the street, a cloud of diesel exhaust from a city bus engulfed him. Maybe that, too, was a sign.

Ron was extremely accurate in his estimate of the phone call. It came about twenty minutes after Tim returned to his dull, sterile, monotonous office overlooking Lake Michigan dotted with diamonds sparkling in the brilliant afternoon sunshine. A voice at the other end of the call told him to be prepared for written employment confirmation. When he asked the name of his new employer, the phone went dead. Strange human relations technique.

TEN

The morning sun smartly popped up over the eastern horizon as if it were on a taut coiled spring. Lake Michigan seemed to take on a more lustrous quality as the dazzling golden orb moved higher in the morning sky. Coffee and croissants started the day at a small shop well hidden by the locals trying to get some relief from the high prices of the tourist and haute couture washing along the glamorous Miracle Mile. Tim left the usual fifty percent tip, waved goodbye at the owner and slid out the side door. The side door was his favorite since it came out in an alley exactly at the same spot the "G-ride" was parked with the blue light on the dash. The "Government Vehicle, aka "G-ride" was one of the enigmas related to the title Special Agent. The car represented free transportation, but it also represented a twenty-four-hour response requirement. Parking was costly, but the microphone over the mirror was a parking pass painfully acknowledged by the voraciously hostile species known as "Parking Enforcement."

The pager on Tim's belt vibrated. He looked at the tiny digital display, *"Area code 202 meant a call from somewhere in the D.C. area."* The number was not familiar, but since he was only a few minutes from the office, he decided to call from his desk. More comfortable, more secure, more time to check the number before calling.

When his official government vehicle was ensconced in its legal and proper spot, Tim trudged to the Dirksen Federal Building. His secure entry card still opened the door, so it appeared he was still employed. Walking through the reception area directly to his office, he started searching a computer database for the owner of the phone number glaring at him from the little window on the pager. After several fruitless minutes, it appeared that the number was unlisted. He called the number.

The sound from the other end was very clear. An androgynous voice softly said, "Hello." No further sounds for several seconds.

Tim waited a few moments and replied, "Hello?"

"Yes, Mister Church. Thank you for your prompt reply. If you would please be at the lobby entrance to the coffee shop in the Royal Carlton Hotel in three hours, one of our associates would like to speak with you. Would that be satisfactory?"

"Yes, I can be there."

The call was terminated in an instant. Tim shuffled some mundane paperwork, stared through the window, and shifted uneasily in his chair. Eventually, the time had come for him to leave for the hotel and a meeting with an unknown person.

ELEVEN

Tim passed through the polished brass and etched glass revolving lobby doors at the hotel and found a comfortable chair with a view of the entrance to the restaurant. The lobby could have been taken directly from an old Bogart movie. Uneasy, Tim watched and waited.

Expecting to meet a man in a dark suit, a snap-brim fedora and a briefcase, Tim was startled when a confident female voice said, "Good morning, Mister Church."

Looking up, he was confronted by a conservatively dressed woman in her forties, with collar-length, salt and pepper hair, high cheek bones, deep brown eyes and slightly freckled skin that could easily dominate either a college classroom or an elegant night at the opera. The silver Gucci wristwatch, gray pearl pendant on a delicate silver chain and small gray pearl earrings complimented the conservatively cut, perfectly tailored medium gray pin-striped suit. He thought, *"This woman could have just walked out of a posh boutique on the Via Veneto in Rome."*

"Tim, if I may call you Tim, my name is Angelina Molinari. If you can spare a few minutes, I should be able to answer some questions. Would that be possible?"

Tim tried to identify an accent or some inflection that might give some clue as to her background, but he found none. "You surprised me. I was expecting a balding, middle-aged man in a dark suit and wing-tipped shoes."

A brief smile stole across her face. "You have questions, and I believe I may have some answers. Shall we go into the coffee shop where we can have a more private conversation?"

The empty restaurant provided the perfect venue. Tim thought, *"She probably chose this hour because it was too late for breakfast, and too early for the lunch crowd."* Angelina and Tim sat at a corner booth far from the kitchen doors. Background music from expertly concealed speakers provided some defense against eavesdroppers. In the old days, the noise would have been adequate to cloak any conversation from prying ears and listening equipment, but times change, and so does technology. Now, background noise can be removed from a recording and microphones are much more efficient. They each ordered coffee, black. He thought, *"Very good, no pretenses with cappuccinos or mocha lattes."* They drank their coffee in silence, soaking up the quiet of the room. No small talk. Just watching and waiting.

Angelina broke the cool silence. "Tim, you should know a few things before any further discussions take place. I have been asked to meet with you to ensure you want to proceed to the next step. I will provide some information that would be totally disavowed if ever repeated." Angelina continued, "You have submitted your resignation to your current employer, and we have updated the resume you submitted some time ago. We have continued to monitor your activities and life events through various means and are satisfied we can continue. I will show you a document. Please read it and return it to me. It is a summary of your information to this point."

She took a manila folder from her leather case, removed the pages and passed them to Tim. He studied the documents, "I see someone has been watching me and collecting information from many sources. Some of the sources must have had some very personal information, or the intercepts were quite good. Of course, much of the information could be obtained from any commercial computer site or combination thereof." Based on the data, he was very certain this group employs hackers to access information touted to be in safe storage. He returned the document to Angelina and waited. She placed the papers in her briefcase, abruptly stood and walked away without a word. Somewhat bewildered, he looked at an envelope resting on the table. He pulled out a document, unfolded it and read the message.

"Welcome to your new career. Please contact our Human Resources Department within twenty-four hours at the telephone number you have been using. You will be provided with complete instructions."

Tim walked back to his office, sat at his gray, metal government-issued desk, and stared out the window.

TWELVE

Tim was hungry. He realized he had been staring out the window too long and was well into the lunch hour. A beer and a sandwich at the all-male stand-up bar at the Berghoff Restaurant around the corner from the Dirksen Building would be a good decision. The public telephones would also be a good placed to make the call to Human Resources. A five-minute walk to the bar brought him to the public telephones ensconced in their original individual booths. He dialed the number, waited two rings, and heard a familiar voice. "Hello Tim, glad you could call," said the voice at the other end. A real voice. It was Ron. "Welcome to your new life. We sent an overnight envelope to your post office box to arrive by ten tomorrow morning. It contains administrative information for your new banking accounts and wire transfer documents indicating the deposit of funds into your current checking account to cover any incidentals you incur in your move to our headquarters office. You will also receive your travel information from Chicago to your new home. Any questions?"

Tim thought for a second. *I have many questions, but they can wait until after I receive the morning package.* Tim spoke into the handset, "Will I see anyone from my new employer before I get to New York?"

"Maybe, but don't worry. You made the right choice. See you soon."

THIRTEEN

The fitful night passed with Tim alternating between bouts of anxious sleep and no sleep at all. The Post Office was moderately busy when he opened his mailbox and found the overnight letter. He opened the envelope containing a single sheet of paper. The page, illuminated by the diffused sunlight coming through the art-deco era windows, revealed the name and phone number of a national moving company, the address of a warehouse in Chicago where his household goods would be placed into temporary storage and a new phone number that would be his contact for travel information. Tim owned a small condo at the end of East Randolph Street overlooking the north shore of Lake Michigan since he had arrived in the city, and now had to decide whether to sell or keep the unit. That decision could come later.

He went to his office and readied himself for the move. Only a few more days before he would turn in his car keys, badge, credentials, and pistol. A few signatures on some government forms, and he would officially retire and start collecting his pension.

FOURTEEN

Less than a week later, the newly retired ATF agent greeted the start of a new month and a new life with an unexpected calm. Tim spent the night at the Royal Carlton Hotel after he had closed his condo, sent his personal belongings to a storage facility, and carried two suitcases containing his entire wardrobe. He was scheduled to meet a private jet at Meigs Field, the lakefront airport just ten minutes from the hotel, in a few hours. Hurry up and wait.

Tim checked out, left his luggage with the concierge for temporary storage, walked into the coffee shop and waited for a table. A moment later, a square-jawed, mature, moderately tall man with close-cropped salt and pepper hair and a sharp, hawk-like nose walked into the restaurant and stood next to Tim. The expensive charcoal slacks, camel cashmere sweater over a black linen shirt, weathered and worn brown US Air Force A-2 leather flying jacket and a pair of highly polished mahogany loafers spoke volumes about the dignified gentleman. The man smiled at Tim and said, "Good morning. Tim. I am Kurt von Richter and I have the distinct pleasure of accompanying you this morning. We will fly several short hours into the morning sun before we arrive at our destination. Our aircraft is equipped with a full galley. The Steward can prepare a decent All-American breakfast, or a

European breakfast of pastries and croissants. The coffee is hot, fresh and the best we can find. Would you care to have breakfast now, or wait until we are airborne?"

Tim thought, *"Kurt has an interesting accent. His English is much too formal to be a natural-born American. He sounds like someone accustomed to speaking 'High-German', with an above average education and breeding who expects his requests will be obeyed."* Tim smiled and nodded, "I can certainly wait until we are on the plane."

"Good, I have a thermos of fresh, hot coffee in our limo. Shall we go?" The driver had already placed Tim's luggage into the shiny, vintage Mercedes ready to make the short journey to the airport.

FIFTEEN

Chicago Meigs Field rests at the shoreline of Lake Michigan a few minutes from the stores, theaters, hotels, and offices bursting up from the area of Chicago known as "The Loop." The airport caters to private aviation and can accommodate small business jets. Just off the north end of the runway lies the Adler Planetarium while the McCormick Place Convention Center guards the approach to the south. Tim watched the driver unload his luggage from the vehicle into the sleek business jet. A moment later, Kurt and Tim walked from the private passenger terminal toward a waiting Cessna Citation Excel, 8 passenger business jet. The bright white and gray paint scheme gleamed as the morning sun rose over a brilliant azure Lake Michigan dotted with millions of diamonds sparkling in the light breeze.

Minutes later, the Cessna smoothly began a climbing right turn to the east and the next chapter of Tim's life. The steward served orange juice, hot coffee and warm croissants with some of the best fruit preserves Tim had ever tasted.

Kurt lounging in a tan leather chair across from Tim opened with the question, "How much do you know about our group?"

Tim peered through the window. "I know it has enough money for an 800 number, a jet and no other real specifics."

The impeccable host countered with, "If you have no knowledge about who we are and what we do, then why did you agree to join?"

"Because I sent a resume to someone at the urging of an old friend."

For just a second, Kurt gave a blank stare, and then allowed acknowledgement to wash across his face. He laughed. "Good answer. One of the better answers to that question. When we arrive at our destination, briefings and orientation will begin, and you will soon know and understand what we do, and how and why we do it."

SIXTEEN

Two hours, and one time zone later, the pilot reduced power for their approach into the Islip, New York airport. The Cessna kissed the runway and taxied to the parking ramp. A white SUV with heavily tinted windows was waiting for them and their luggage. The bags were deftly deposited into the SUV by a tall, trim, muscled driver with intelligent green eyes, a short, but fashionable haircut, casual, but expensive jeans, sweater and leather jacket. *Leather jackets must be the uniform.* Tim thought, *"No talk. Just get into the ride and watch the Long Island scenery go by."*

Eventually, they turned onto a short entrance road quickly blocked by a ten-foot-high wrought iron fence. The driver pressed a button on the SUV console, and the gates quietly and effortlessly slid to the side allowing the vehicle passage through a stand of old growth trees. The road snaked through the woods on a path designed to keep a vehicle at less than jogging speed with strategically placed iron barriers alongside the road. Suddenly, a large stone structure burst into view across a meadow. It looked like a small college with two tiers of windows multiple chimneys and a peaked roof, the quintessential Long Island mansion. As they drove closer to the house, the road eased uphill to a crest where the remainder of the property came into view. A large expanse of lush, green manicured lawn drew his eyes to a view of the azure ocean covering the Block Island Shelf leading out to the Atlantic. Today the calm water in front of him was in stark contrast with the turmoil in his gut. His thoughts were broken when the SUV came to a stop. The building was much more substantial than his first impression and exuded massive wealth and entitlement. A chill coursed through his body as they left the warmth of the SUV and walked the few steps to the impressive entrance.

A man of indeterminate age immediately opened the door and greeted them by name. "Hello Kurt. Welcome Tim. I am Conrad von Junginen. Welcome to The Directorate and our modest, but efficient, surroundings." A slight bow replaced the standard handshake. The man before him appeared to be a bit older than Kurt, with a slight frame, pale skin, balding pate and the demeanor of someone who has always been comfortable with great wealth and power. Tim thought, *"This guy could blend into nearly any crowd at a university library book reading event. Conrad, like Kurt, spoke in perfect American English, but with an old German or Austrian nuance. He could have been right out of 'Central Casting' as an old Prussian Count, or a highly experienced butler."*

Stepping aside, Conrad continued, "This is where you will maintain a permanent residence while you are part of our group. Kurt, please show our newest colleague to his quarters. We will all meet in an hour in the library to share information about how we can move forward together."

Kurt led Tim through a foyer and into a large similarly paneled hallway hung with oil paintings and surveillance cameras along its entire length. The corridor terminated at a large, double, floor to ceiling window providing a view of more trees and beautifully manicured lush, green lawn. Kurt turned to a wooden panel, slid a piece of the wainscot to the side, and stepped back as a panel moved to reveal a polished stainless-steel elevator door. The door opened to an elevator large enough to carry ten people. When the elevator door closed Kurt said, "Three, please." A disembodied female voice with a slightly British accent said, "Thank you, Kurt."

A few seconds later, the door opened to a modern hallway lined with cork material and dull, brushed nickel enhancements. Highly polished wood flooring became a sounding board for their footsteps, while subdued lighting gave a comfortable glow to their pathway. Kurt made a right turn out of the elevator and walked along the hall to a set of double doors complete with a cipher lock, retinal imaging and fingerprint scanner. He went through the machinations, and the doors unlocked.

Tim followed Kurt through the open electronic portal. The men went about four steps into the room, when Kurt stopped and turned to face Tim. "This is your new home. You will have other places to stay, but this will be your permanent residence for as long as you are with the group. The locks are for your safety. They keep others out of your little place of respite, and let you relax, restore, and rejuvenate. The locks have been keyed to me so that I can show you this apartment. After our meeting, everything will change to you. Take some time to unwind and explore the amenities of your new home. The elevator has been programed to allow your return to the main floor. Tim walked around his new home. A sitting room, bedroom, bath, walk-in closet, kitchen, and a great view of the ocean, all crammed into about three thousand square feet comprised his "castle within the castle." Not too bad. Tim looked at a diagram of the building on the wall next to the door. He would need the information to find the library.

SEVENTEEN

The library door was open. Six people were seated in green leather armchairs around a mahogany table inlaid with lighter shades of zebra wood. Zebra Wood has the distinction of being the most expensive hardwood in the world. An exotic wood with an appearance that resembles the striping of the animal with the same name, also used inside luxury cars and Prada's flagship store in Manhattan. Tim thought, *Interesting choice since it is from an endangered tree in West Africa. This could be a clue to the societal values of the group as well as reinforcing its appearance of opulence.*

Tall windows with heavy, dark green drapes provided a path for muted rays of light in a soft autumn hue. Leather bound books lined three of the walls on teak-wood shelves with a ladder meant to slide along the face to access the upper rows. Very collegial. Very traditional. Very expensive.

Tim entered the room noting the one unoccupied chair immediately to the right of Conrad. As soon as Tim cleared the threshold, the door closed with the soft click of an electronic lock, and metal panels silently lowered to completely cover the windows. He was now in a closed vault. Tim took the remaining chair and waited for something to happen. Conrad began, "As you know, we have a new addition to our group. Since all of you had a hand in the selection process, I will dispense with the banalities of a welcoming speech other than to thank Tim for accepting our invitation to help with our current and future plans."

Tim looked around the table and found confident, friendly faces. He knew Ron from Viet Nam, but he knew nothing of the others.

Speaking to the group Conrad said, "I believe we should briefly introduce Tim to our mission, members and activities." Turning to face Tim he continued, "Tim, we are a small, cohesive group working to correct affronts and outrages to the common good of society as instructed by our directors. When individuals or groups act in a manner contrary to human decency and the interests of our directors, we are tasked to prevent, halt, or correct that action. We have ample resources to assist in this endeavor, regardless of political, cultural, or financial boundaries. In other words, we work when and where we please without being shackled by political or legal convention. For example, when a group wishes to destabilize a legally and ethically formed government, we combat that aggression, regardless of the source or nature of the destabilization. When greed results in harm to those who cannot defend themselves, we provide the necessary aid to those people. You will begin your introduction to our world after we conclude our evening meal. Ron will be your sponsor during the initial process, but please become acquainted with your colleagues as soon as possible. Never forget that the positive results of our actions are tied directly to the good of our directors. But no matter the result, our directors shall never lose."

Tim considered what had just been said. *We do good, but our directors never lose. These tenets may not be compatible. What was that about?* Before he could formulate an answer to himself, he saw the lone woman at the table watching him. He was about to say something to Angelina, but she shifted her eyes toward Kurt.

Conrad rose from his seat at the head of the table. Even though it was a round table, Tim thought it was quite apparent that Conrad was *First among equals*. The neo-Prussian quickly disappeared through a doorway concealed behind a sliding section of wall paneling.

The remaining members of the group sat quietly and waited. After a long pause, Kurt looked directly at Tim, and began speaking with a voice that belied a subtle Maryland Eastern Shore accent with hints of Imperial Europe. "You are about to learn things that you may not immediately comprehend, but I assure you that what you hear is quite true. What you will see is quite true. What you will experience is the result of past actions, and non-actions, of this group over many years. Just remember, this group has changed personnel over the years, but the mission has never changed.

For example, the Directorate faced a difficult set of circumstances during the late 1930's when the world was involved in a near global conflict. The directors had expected the war to occur and formed business partnerships and alliances with both sides of the conflict to guarantee and improve their financial positions. Our predecessors, however, discovered a potential threat to the status quo when one of their assets, a British double agent, received a request from the Germans to obtain the operational plan used by the British to successfully attack Taranto, Italy, the primary Italian Navy port in the Mediterranean. According to the Germans, the Japanese had been impressed by the attack and asked their ally to help secure the British operational plans. The Japanese had been contemplating an attack on the United States, a country deemed 'weak' by the Japanese Imperial Staff. When the double agent received the request, he contacted his British handlers. The British notified the Americans and sent their agent to Washington to provide the details to the United States War Department and the FBI. The egotistical military commanders mired in World War I ideology dismissed the Japanese plan and chose to ignore the warning. When the double agent was sent to the FBI, Mister Hoover refused to see the Brit on at least two occasions and threw him out of FBI Headquarters after the third attempt. Apparently, the double agent was also known as a gambler, drinker and a womanizer, all repugnant qualities to Hoover. The Brit tried to warn the War Department but met with a similar fate. They ignored his warnings. When the directors learned of the United States inaction, they made the appropriate business and political moves to ensure success as they did business with both sides of the inevitable conflict and secured increased war profits and financial power. The directors had tried to contain the war, but arrogant and inept politicians and bureaucrats could not be persuaded to act. So, the world suffered, but the Directorate did well."

Tim leaned back in his chair, "I guess things have not really changed in sixty years. The bureaucrats and politicians continue to wear blinders to maintain their dreary existence."

Kurt allowed a slight smile to creep across his face, even to his eyes. Tim had seen smiling faces with stone cold eyes, but Kurt did not exhibit that look. It was more of an intensely serious smile.

Then Ron Johnson stood up, turned to Kurt and said, "We all know Conrad is the direct line from the Main Office. He is our team manager who gives us our assignments and provides us with direct support when we need it. He is very good at what he does, but he is not a field operative, nor does he have any specialized scientific, technical or legal credentials. He will be your best friend when you think you are out of options and your worst enemy when you don't need one."

Tim stole a glance at Kurt who briefly smiled but did not protest the description.

Ron then introduced the rest of the group. Tim already knew Ron, or thought he did. The former Navigator described his journey through life to this point with little flair. Only statement after statement with few details. A typical briefing outline. It seems that upon leaving Viet Nam, he continued his career with Air Force Intelligence and built up a prestigious resume as an analyst. After doing his time in the Air Force, he moved to the civilian side of the intelligence world. He stayed with a clandestine agency until he had had enough of their peacetime program with its politics. He made contacts on the civilian contractor side of the system and earned some good money. One night, he was watching a Bruins-Blackhawks hockey game at the Chicago Stadium when a guy seated next to him started a conversation. Kurt recruited Ron on the spot and he has been with the group since.

Next was Ingrid Powers, who had played the part of Angelina. Ron turned toward Ingrid. Today she was dressed in charcoal gray slacks and a dark claret, crew neck cashmere sweater. No jewelry. Hair neatly tied at the nape of her neck.

Ron began, "Ingrid was born in Lincoln, Nebraska. The only child of Joseph and Francesca Powers. She attended public schools in her hometown until moving to California and studied Psychology at Stanford where she graduated Magna Cum Laude with a Bachelor of Science. She went on to Yale for her Masters' and a PhD in Clinical Behavioral Science. After several years on staff at Massachusetts General Hospital followed by a stint at Johns Hopkins, she joined our friends at the CIA working in the Behavioral Science group as a Profiler in the counter-intelligence field. She looked for potential and actual security threats in people and the system. You might call her our 'Internal Affairs' and 'psychological profiler for our assets and the other side. She tries to ferret out any security problems. During her first year at Stanford, her parents were killed by a sleepy semi-truck driver in an auto accident just west of Omaha. She speaks fluent French, Italian and American English, with a smattering of assorted Eastern European and North African languages. Seven years ago, we recruited Ingrid from the doldrums of government life, and she has never looked back."

Tim thought, *Apparently, she had never found the right man because her left ring finger was conspicuously devoid of any jewelry.*

Ron looked to his right and nodded at a youngish man replete in the rigid uniform of disaffected youth with collar length dirty blonde hair, an acne scarred round face, wire rimmed glasses, a very faded black Grateful Dead T-shirt, khaki cargo shorts and sandals. This young specimen could have been on the cover of *Computer Geek and Cheetos Magazine.*

"This is "Eddie" aka Edward James Braden III. Eddie is our resident Technical Operations Manager. He will change your lock settings, provide you with any tech support equipment and knowledge required both in the field and here at home. He can also get your VCR to work with the remote and unlock your computer when necessary. He has a background in Computer Science, fraud, digital theft, and several other little hobbies. He should be finishing his fourth year in the graduate program at the Terre Haute Federal Penitentiary, but as fortune would have it, he is 'with us' or 'belongs to us' we are never really quite sure." Eddie gave a huge smile that could melt the heart of the coldest sixth grade teacher. But an impish, evil grin flashed across his face as he momentarily stared at Ingrid.

"Our final member is Hugh Carrick Farrell. Hugh is our primary Field Operations Officer. He has many talents we find useful in situations where boardroom negotiations, civility and diplomatic options have become untenable. Hugh is fluent in several Middle Eastern languages, French, Mandarin, and German. You and Hugh will become more acquainted as you move forward in your career with this group. Born at Belfast, Northern Ireland to an Irish father and a Saudi mother, he served with the British Army in Operation Banner. He encountered some unfortunate difficulties and left the Queen's service after his term of enlistment expired. Weapons, explosives, communications, combat medicine and personal combat techniques are some of his skills. Diplomacy and ethics are included lesser features in his portfolio." Hugh flashed a malevolent smile with eyes that hurtled from high intelligence to two pieces of granite devoid of any human emotion.

Tim momentarily considered this final member of the team seated at the table. He was something straight out of the movies if you were looking for a physical, taut, unnerving, emotionless automaton with short hair, steel gray eyes, strong chin, and muscles upon muscles beneath the black tee shirt. Tim considered the man and thought, *Very scary. I can only guess at his talents. He seems to be breathing, but I may be wrong.*

Ron looked directly at Tim and said, "Now we come to you and why you are here. You may have noted that we have quite an array of ages, experience and knowledge in this room. Any skills and competences not represented in this room are obtained through specific vendors. Over the years, you have acquired a set of proficiencies, demeanor, and a quality we believe can be useful. Please know that you replace someone who was more than an asset to the group. He was a friend. I will only satisfy your natural curiosity by saying that he earned his retirement years, and will unreservedly enjoy them with the same panache, courage and aplomb that served him through his time with the group. When you submitted your resume to us, you were already on our radar as a potential addition to the group. The resume you submitted served as an indication of your interest and willingness to serve in a unique capacity. When deemed necessary to contact you, we were already certain you would accept.

In general, your position within the group will utilize the talents and expertise you have gained in both your professional and personal lives. You will assume the role of 'everyman' in our operations. Hugh could never play that role, and the wrong people are too familiar with me to be effective for much longer. While your primary function will be managerial, you will also be tasked to join field operations as required. You will assist Ingrid with 'counter-intelligence' as the 'field operative' and any other assistance she may need. The details of your role will become apparent as you study our previous accomplishments and failures. Yes, we have failed on several occasions, and you will certainly recognize those failures when you review the files during your training period." Ron looked at Kurt, "We need a break. We'll go to the great hall where staff has provided light snacks and beverages."

EIGHTEEN

The group moved out of the library through a corridor lined with paintings of men and women who appeared to be from various eras back to the 1700's. Tim recognized a few of them as noted military, political and financial leaders who were not always on the same side of a dispute or cause. Interesting mix. They all had vast wealth, or power, or both. History had judged some of them rather harshly. But then, history is written by the winner, and to paraphrase Gustave Flaubert, "Truth is only a perception."

The Great Hall was replete with more crystal chandeliers, heavy furniture, highly polished parquet flooring and an array of foods that would rival any repast in a world traveler magazine. Tim wondered if this would be a regular experience, or would hot dogs and hamburgers be served on paper plates at the next gathering.

Moments later, Conrad came into the room looking pensive. He stopped near the sideboard loaded with caviar and pate and said, "Ladies and gentlemen. We may have a situation. One of our assets provided some information that could be quite unsettling to the Directors. After we take refreshments, we shall return to the library. Please enjoy."

Immediately following the meal, Tim waylaid Ron in the hallway. "Ron. I believe you totally failed to fully introduce

Kurt, and only slightly mentioned Conrad. Is there a reason for this?"

Ron looked up and down the hallway. "I'll brief you later. Let's get into the library."

The group met in the library where Conrad was already seated in his chair. He pushed a button below the edge of the tabletop, and a section of paneled wall slid open revealing a large video screen. As he began to speak, a photo of a seaport teeming with various civilian and military ships filled the screen. "This is the port of Aden, Yemen. In several weeks, the USS Donovan, an Arleigh Burke-class guided missile destroyer is scheduled to visit the port. We have just intercepted information judged to have a high confidence level by the US Department of Defense Intelligence Service and the Deputy of Central Intelligence. They believe the ship has been targeted by Al-Qaeda. Our own intelligence sources verified the group intends to load a small boat with explosives, sail as close as possible to the Donovan, and detonate the cargo hoping to sink the ship. They plan to blend in with harbor taxis, delivery boats and general marine traffic to make a run at the Donovan before anyone can react. We have already identified the leaders in this attempt and are tracking their communications, and physical and financial moves. At this point, both DoD and DCI lack information specifically from our sources. Directorate leadership determined this attack will be too destabilizing to their political and financial positions to be allowed. At the conclusion of this briefing, each of you will be provided with your tasks in this operation. Any questions? No? Good."

Conrad then rose from his chair and disappeared through the doorway behind the paneling.

The members of the group looked at each other. Tim must have looked a bit uncertain because both Kurt and Ron came over to him. Kurt said, "You have been assigned to assist Ron with this operation. He will mentor you for now. At some point, you will be trained by each member of the group until you have learned every position."

Kurt left the room and started down the hallway. Ron said, "Welcome to your new world. You will see, hear and do things you have not imagined, or maybe you have." His face then opened to an ominous smile. "It's show-time."

They walked to a wall of bookshelves. Ron put his hand on a book lying flat on a shelf. The bookcase slid to the side revealing an austere, antiseptic corridor with a single steel door at the far end. They walked out of the room along the corridor. Upon reaching the end of the passage, the door automatically opened to a room filled with wall-mounted video screens, light gray acoustically padded walls, recessed lighting, and computer consoles. The sounds were just above a whisper, even though four other people were either speaking normally into headsets or having conversations. They had entered the "command and control" center. Ron led Tim to a console near the center of the room.

"What do you think of your new office?" Ron asked. "Gives the appearance of a Spartan operation, but this is only the control center for a vast network of people, equipment and resources. We collect intelligence information from many sources and technologies. This room is the ultimate terminus. Some sources are unaware of our ability to capture their work product, but that has been the nature of the group throughout its history. Clandestine operations are our forte."

The displays were amazing. This group had access to information far beyond the reach of most governments. He stood still, watched, and listened, overwhelmed by the operation.

Ron eased into a chair parked in front of a console with several video monitors. "Let's get to work." Ron opened and reviewed scores of screen images over the next hour. Tim, looking over his shoulder, saw photos of people, places, documents, boats, trucks, automobiles, remote runways, what appeared to be seismic graphs, and the current National Hockey League Central Division schedule.

Tim leaned forward, pointed to the screen image that looked like the seismic graph shown on TV after an earthquake, and asked, "What is that all about?"

Ron smiled, rubbed the back of his neck, and quietly responded, "These are results of a US National Reconnaissance Organization satellite laser scan of a remote desert area in the southern Empty Quarter between Yemen and Saudi Arabia. The satellite uses a laser to search up to thirty feet below the surface for any anomalies, such as metallic objects, underground structures and certain chemical and nuclear signatures. Interestingly, several years ago NRO discovered long forgotten and obscured portions of the "Spice Road" in the Empty Quarter of the Arabian Peninsula using laser surveillance satellite technology. They attributed the discovery to commercial satellite images from space, but that was the cover story. We hack into their computers, 'liberate' the data and use the information without their knowledge."

Ron studied the next screen displaying a photograph of a Middle Eastern male. Tim asked, "Who is this?" Ron rubbed his eyes, looked at the screen again. "This is Abd Al-Rahim al-Nashiri. Our sources insist he is the mastermind behind a series of potential Millennium plots to be executed within the next weeks. Those sources, and our internal interpretation of the information at hand, indicates they will execute their plans on December 31. The Middle East targets will be in the Kingdom of Jordan, and include the Radisson Hotel in Amman, Mount Nebo, and a site on the Jordan river where John the Baptist is said to have baptized Jesus. In addition to those sites, the Los Angeles International Airport is targeted with a nitroglycerine attack. Conrad interrupted our little meeting this afternoon because these attacks were not scheduled to happen until New Years' Eve. We massaged the information, reached out to some assets, and determined their updated schedule. The new date was confirmed this afternoon by a human asset within the organization. No suitable substitute for a real, live person."

Tim studied the face on the screen. The eyes were clear, dark, and completely devoid of any emotion. Not the eerily, serene look of one who has come to accept finality, but the face of a calculating individual devoid of any humanity. This individual would not give up his worldly existence but would be more than willing to send others to that fate. Again. And again. And again. It was not a gaunt face, but a thin appearance like many of those who follow a Spartan regimen. It was a face like many Bedouin faces. One that could hide in plain view in any Arab population. This would be a difficult target. But not impossible.

Tim suggested, "Maybe he will commit the one mistake eventually made by everyone. Do we have eyes on him, or any hard intel on his actions?"

A new screen popped up. A satellite image of a group of buildings in a barren, desert landscape northwest of Aden, Yemen. The buildings appeared to be nothing more than a few old, abandoned mud structures at the end of an ancient trail. Ron pressed a computer key and the image changed. It was the same general view, but the colors of the image had changed. Three markers snapped into view with an arrow pointing to the center of two of the buildings, and another to an open area a few meters from a large rock. A few more keystrokes, and the right side of the screen was filled with a column of what appeared to be chemical formulas. Another set of keystrokes, and the formulas changed to text. A list of chemical names. He smiled and called to the others in a casual voice, "I think we have something over here."

Ingrid, Hugh, and Eddie immediately came to their console. Grim smiles all around. Tim thought, *What was happening?* Before he could ask the question aloud, Ron blurted, "Looks like we found the treasure. The success rate for this source is about ninety per cent. Now we can do some business." He turned and said, "Tim, this is a satellite feed from one of the birds in an orbit over our suspected target area and is the result of satellite-based laser ground penetrating technology. While radar images are commonly known to be used in the intelligence community for locating certain targets at ground level, this laser technology owned by one of our government assets can also locate substances below the surface, analyze the chemical composition and display it in both chemical formulas and common names. The laser pulses energy to the ground and transmits the information back to the receiver, where it is processed, decoded and transmitted to the proper addressee." Ron shrugged and smiled impishly, "We hack into the system and the information is sent directly to us, and no one else. The owners have no idea that the laser found anything. This station is the only recipient and right now, the owner is trying to determine why this satellite changed its orbit ever so slightly. So, what do you think we have here?"

Tim studied the screen. "Looks like we have three targets consisting of multiple chemical compounds. Two of the targets are in the buildings, and one is here in an open area by a rock. I don't know what the rest of it means."

"Good start," came a voice from behind Tim. Eddie Braden had a smirk on his face. It was the kind of look a nerd with a "death wish" wears when he feels superior to the inferior minions of the universe. That expression was usually the last thing on his face just before the nerd was unceremoniously placed head-first into a toilet by some jock.

"Thanks for the kind words, Eddie," Tim replied. "My knowledge of lasers is limited to using them when I dropped five-hundred-pound laser-guided bombs from my fighter into the window of a building next to an orphanage in the center of a city."

Hugh laughed. "Nice one! Well, Eddie, looks like you made a new friend. Remember, he used to put people like you in jail for a long time. Maybe he can still do that. I, on the other hand, will just break your fingers so you will never use a keyboard again. Would you like that?" The speed and viciousness of the words were like a lightning bolt, but no one showed any sign of surprise.

They all returned their attention to the screen. While the rest of the group studied the display, Tim waited for his training to start. Ron entered a few more keystrokes, and the image displayed an overlay with latitude and longitude, accompanied by sharper terrain relief, but no target symbols or chemical notations.

Eddie started, "Ron has just brought up images from a pass the same bird made twenty-four hours ago. As you can see, there were no identified laser targets. The map coordinates verify this is the same location, but there are no targets. This confirms information supplied by one of our assets within their organization. The source claimed that fighters loyal to al-Nashiri had brought a large cache of explosives to this storage location for eventual use in Yemen. The laser confirms the exact type and location of the chemicals. Our chemical library for this laser includes the chemicals used in the explosives, PETN and RDX. The computer program analyzes the chemicals and compares the results to the data stored in the computer program library. The results are displayed on the screen as the final product. In this case, calculations indicate the explosive, SEMTEX, a very popular item from the former Eastern Bloc countries. Data indicates this is a high quality, commercially manufactured compound, not something made at a kitchen table. That's it for now."

Tim leaned toward Ron and said. "When will you have time to give me the info on Kurt and Conrad?"

Ron leaned back in his chair, "When we finish here, we can take a walk around the grounds. You need to know what we have outside this building." The former navigator returned to his computer screen and worked for the next two hours with Tim in the role of an observer.

NINETEEN

Half a world to the east a group of men gathered where a hazy late summer sky obscured the pale, morning sun as it rose over Kuala Lumpur, the capital city of Malaysia, and the meeting location chosen by Jalil, known as the "Professor", and the current operational director of Al Qaeda. The small, dingy white hotel, nestled among other vintage buildings from the British colonial period, was the meeting site for three men planning their boldest venture intended to bring the infidels to their knees. "The Professor" joined with his associates, Fahd, "The Panther" and Khallad, "The Chechen", to form the group tasked to develop and execute bombings at two sites in Jordan, the Los Angeles International Airport and Aden, Yemen to coincide with the pending Millenium.

Jalil spoke firmly, but quietly, "We have come this far, and we shall not fail in our endeavor. But, to ensure success we must have the necessary funds to mount this effort. Khallad, have you made progress with the Arab bin Alkanor, a member of the Directorate?"

Khallad looked at both men, "Yes, Alkanor has guaranteed his nephew Prince Ibn Al Wahidi will provide us with sufficient funds to complete our plans. The old man demands his role in this matter must remain a total secret. He fears retribution by the other members of the Directorate if they discover his role in this operation. They are not motivated by seeking glory through Allah, but through worldly riches and power."

Fahd leaned forward, "If they are not true believers, can we trust them?"

Khallad smiled, "They are not believers and are afraid of losing their wealth, power, and lives. I have dealt with their kind in the past. They will not hesitate to provide funds if they fear me. I have given them adequate incentives. I reminded them of the fate of some of their family members. They have made a poor choice and now fear their own families and us. The young prince wants to be king, but others in the royal succession have other ideas. He tries to be ruthless, but he is a privileged coward."

Jalil quietly interrupted, "When may we expect to receive additional funds?"

Khallad sighed, "I will be speaking with Alkanor in a few hours. Our emissary is ready to receive the cash. We will use the same plan for the funds."

"Excellent, Khallad, now we must move on to our projects. We have been sowing doubt and fear inside America, but we need to increase our efforts. Do we still have the same contacts in the news media and the greedy politicians?"

"Yes. We have additional recruits in several locations including airports and airlines We expect to have more eyes and ears supporting our plans."

"Do you know if the young prince is still secure within this group known as the 'Directorate' or the royal family?"

"We do not have anyone inside the Directorate, but one or two royal family members are somewhat suspicious. Our spies will inform us if anything changes. The Directorate is another matter. They can be quite effective, and difficult."

TWENTY

The day had been quite full for Tim when Ron led them through multi-paned, French doors on the south side of the building to an enormous carpet of grass stretching to the beach and the cold waters of the Atlantic. Majestic, mature maple and Eastern Red Cedar trees combined with barbed shrubbery formed barriers on each side of the property concealing the metal security fencing and sensors liberally placed along the perimeter. Ron sat on one of the dark green, wooden benches near the beach strategically placed on the small meadow to provide maximum separation from actual and potential listening devices and motioned for Tim to join him.

Tim turned to Ron, "Tell me about Kurt."

The former navigator looked over his shoulder at the mansion. "He has impeccable credentials if you like someone who worked for the Stasi, the East German Secret Police, at their Berlin Headquarters before German re-unification. Our records show that he was one of the most successful and feared East German Agents. Funny thing, the Agency and the Bureau have decent records on him, but not as a direct threat to the US. He was the head of the section that worked on the Russians. The Russians really hated him, and in some circles they most likely still do. Condescension, failure to recognize change and arrogance throughout US civilian and military intelligence lead these people to believe we were the greatest thorn in Russia's side, but the Soviets could not totally control the Stasi. Kurt operated a group of spies embedded deep within the KGB, stealing information from the highest levels of the Soviet Government. The Russians and Germans have never really been friends, and the carnage Russia visited on the Germans at the end of World War II cemented that attitude. His family goes back a long way to the old Duchy of Prussia. I think his family and Conrad's family both held high rank as far back as the 1500's in a group known as the 'Teutonic Knights.' He has many skills, but treachery is his finest and most developed. Never give him a reason to use his skills on you, and believe me, he will use them if he deems it in his best interests. Kurt was once married for several years but lost his family in a house explosion and fire. He believes his family was killed by the Russians sending him a message, and all factors point to that as the truth. He has few, if any, friends but many enemies. The rest of society is just background noise in his world. In his eyes, his only real peer is Conrad. But they are more like cooperating factions using each other to their own end. 'The end justifies the means' is probably his mantra. Power, wealth, control and retribution seem to be his best descriptors. If asked, I would bet he was collecting a paycheck from our side while he was working for the East Germans."

Ron shifted position on the hard, wooden bench, and furtively looked around the open expanse and continued, "Now for Conrad. He is the eldest nephew of one of the managing directors and has been with the Directorate for nearly thirty years. He came into the group as a 'financial crimes' asset, probably because his ancestors had committed so many financial crimes to grab and hold their wealth. As I said, his family goes back to feudal Prussia and the Teutonic Knights. Records indicate he is related to Konrad von Jungingen, Grandmaster of the Teutonic Knights in the 15th Century. During his tenure, the Knights rose to the peak of their power and influence. Our Conrad comes across as rather 'bookish' and 'unassertive', but he can be very 'severe' when required. He is extremely intelligent, cunning, and ruthless. He is not a field agent, but he is extremely competent at managing operations and the necessary resources. Don't underestimate him." Fittingly, the sun had just dropped behind the western tree line signaling an end to the day, and the briefing.

TWENTY-ONE

The Las Vegas Strip was quiet, but that was typical at four o'clock in the morning. Few lights were on in the hotel rooms of the decadent Western Sodom and Gomorrah. The young Arab man believed Allah would surely and completely destroy this place of sin and shame, but the young prince would like Him to wait a few hours before the extreme annihilation. He still had a bit of drinking, gambling, women and drugs on his schedule. Wearing nothing but a towel, he stood at the giant window overlooking the empty desert while the three young women hastily grabbed their clothes and fled the penthouse. The encoded satellite phone had rudely disrupted the early morning debauchery, and he was not happy. The room door clicked shut, and the man went back to the call. Angrily, he shouted into the phone, "What do you mean you need more money? I provided you with millions, and now you have the nerve to ask for more!"

The metallic voice did not hesitate and shot back, "You want results, but you do not want to be involved or take any chances. This work is not cheap, and I am not cheap. Maybe you would like to personally do the dirty work? I think not. Shall I explain our dilemma to your father or your uncles? I am certain you and your uncle have discussed this matter with your father. Again, I think not. Make the transfer by noon tomorrow, New York time." The line went dead.

The young prince looked at the phone, uttered a Bedouin curse then dialed a number. An agitated, mature voice resonated, "What do you want! I am about to begin my morning prayers."

"Uncle, our mutual friend called and demanded more money. He threatened to abandon the task if we do not provide more funds in the next four hours."

The furious man spat into the phone in a frenzy, "You young fool! I warned you about these men, but you want to demonstrate your power and cunning to the others. The Directorate is not filled with fools, especially Kurt and Conrad. Are you at a hotel in Las Vegas? I told you not to go anywhere you might expose us. I will make the necessary arrangements. You will return to your father's home immediately and stay there until I tell you to do otherwise. I never should have agreed to your plan, but now I must finish and hope we are not killed. Now, do as you are told." The old man was worried. He wanted to claim more power within the Directorate and the family and thought he could use his impetuous royal nephew as a shield. They were playing a dangerous game. The other members would not look kindly on this power grab if they ever discovered the plot. The prince was allowed into the Directorate because of his impeccable educational credentials, his position in his family and his access to vast financial assets. The current directors also believed he was inexperienced and would be easily manipulated. The old uncle sighed, turned to the east and began his morning prayers hoping he could somehow get this done without anyone discovering his part in the operation. If the operation was successful, he would reap millions from oil futures. If the operation failed and he was discovered, he would reap a slow, grisly end to his miserable existence.

A young government employee sat at his console in a small cubicle deep inside a large structure on the grounds of Fort Meade, Maryland. Recently separated from the Army, this young civilian employee was tasked to monitor the equipment processing intercepted electronic data including encoded voice transmissions. About an hour before his shift ended, an alert came across his computer screen. He went through the necessary keystrokes and sent the special communication to its next stop for further processing. A few minutes later, another alert involving the same satellite phone resulted in a like response. Two alerts from the same number in rapid succession was not unusual, but it was noteworthy.

At the same time a young man seated in a room inside a Long Island, New York mansion received a notification on his computer screen. He processed the communications in his system without Fort Meade having any knowledge of the action. The highlighted keywords and subscriber information was of keen interest to his employers.

TWENTY-TWO

Freezing temperatures, few clouds, light winds and unlimited visibility greeted Tim as he began the day. Inside the control room the temperature was cool, the humidity was low, but the atmosphere in the room was as hot as a steel mill furnace. The team knew where the explosives were secreted, the target, the date and some of the players. Their asset inside the terrorist organization was scheduled to send an update within the next several hours. The Directorate had already lost three human assets inside the extremist network, and no one was certain this asset would make contact. Each member went through his or her list of regular resources, searching for any scrap of information that could be linked to any other minute scrap of information, to create a nexus that might result in a potential conclusion with a "high level of confidence." Never a certainty, only a declaration of "high confidence." That is the intelligence business. "High Confidence" is a term that means the "Best Possible Guess." Always hedging their bets.

The digital clock on the sound-proofed wall glowed a red 1641 hours at the location of the asset. 0741 hours at the control room. Tim sat at his newly assigned workstation and stared at his computer monitor thinking about the operation. Since he was in training, several of his computer screens were linked directly to Ron. Tim stretched, leaned to the left, then right and thought. *Maybe the asset will be able to transmit the information needed by the group. Time for another coffee. Seems like my life as an adult has revolved around a coffee cup. Better than a bottle or a synthetic or organic compound. Coffee has never been a disqualifying factor on a blood test determining whether someone will get their next paycheck, a dismissal or worse.*

Eddie walked out from behind his array of consoles. "We have a message from the desert." He handed the hard copy of the text message to Kurt who entered it into a decoding program at a separate computer.

When the coded information was massaged, clear text emerged.

The group surrounded the computer on Kurt's desk. The clear text message popped onto the screen. "2344N seeks 18 M dhow with motor." Kurt quietly remarked, "It appears our Al Qaeda friend, al-Nashiri, wants a fifty-foot wooden boat with a motor." The dhow is a generic term for the ubiquitous boat used in the Red Sea by fishermen and merchants delivering their wares. A single dhow could blend in with the hundreds of other similar craft plying the waters of the Arabian Sea or the Gulf of Aden. The craft is as common as a Chevy or Ford pickup truck in Iowa. This one, however, would have a cargo of explosives. Enough explosives to sink a United States Navy, Man-of-War.

Ingrid had been quietly lingering in the shadows since Tim had arrived, and he wondered why. She sat quietly in front of her computer and endlessly worked the keyboard. Tim had interacted briefly with everyone else, but not Ingrid. Finally, she came over to Tim and Ron. "Ron, Tim, here are the funding routes for the Delta Project," the code for the *USS Donovan* operation. "The money trail started with a Directorate member who is one of the sons of the royal family that has been playing both sides. The boy has some real serious authority issues with his father."

Ron leaned back in his chair calmly noting, "You know, we have some of the same arrogant, privileged types right here in the States. This is an equal opportunity world of 'assholes' where everyone has a chance to make it to the top of the list, and I have personally met a few of them." Ingrid looked at him, smiled coyly, turned on her heels, and went to the kitchen for a snack to maintain her metabolic rate at a satisfactory level.

TWENTY-THREE

Abd Al-Rahim al-Nashiri, the leader of the plot to bomb the USS Donovan pored over satellite photos and assorted diagrams at a large metal table. He had been tasked by Al Qaeda to develop and execute the plot to use explosives to sink the warship as she refueled at the Port of Aden, Yemen. This day, he was staying in a house at the south end of the Afghan Hindu Kush Mountains west of the Khyber Pass, his fourth location in as many days. Security required the nightly moves using different modes of travel.

Nashiri had been a loyal Al Qaeda follower since 1977 and was now a trusted lieutenant to Osama bin Laden. Bin Laden, seated across the table was not comfortable with the choice of the two men chosen by his lieutenant. "Nashiri, why do you use these men? I do not trust them."

"My friend, I know you live by your wits, and have been very successful, but I have every confidence in them. They have been with me for many years and gotten me through many difficult times."

"You have served our cause well and have always triumphed, so I must trust your judgement. But please be careful. Your plan is quite complex and has many places to stumble. But we both know our foe is arrogant and makes many mistakes. May Allah be with you."

Osama walked out of the room, leaving the door open for al-Nashiri's bodyguards to join him at the table. The older man asked softly, "Is everything in order?" The man was not questioning him, but gently asking if all was well.

"Yes, all is well. Osama has some fears about our team in Aden, but he always has fears about something. That is why he is still alive. I think we should have some chai."

His target, the USS Donovan, a US Navy frigate was scheduled to visit the Port of Aden in December. Although the visit to Yemen was classified, the Port had been provided with a loose schedule to ensure adequate provisions would be available to the ship and its crew. Local officials and businesses aware of the approximate date included two Al-Qaeda sympathizers who regularly passed information to the Al Qaeda network of informers. Al-Nashiri usually worked alone but was not averse to using other sources during the planning process. Speaking to his bodyguards, he confided, "The ship will be most vulnerable during the morning hours when the port would be congested with normal commercial vessels. I must find a dhow." This commonly used wooden fishing and cargo vessel that constituted a majority of port traffic would melt into the morning throng of vessels crowding the waters of the port. "My plan is quite simple. A single dhow will be invisible among the mass of small craft. The boat shall carry enough explosives to blast a large hole in the side the warship at the waterline. The crew will simply pull alongside the ship as if ready to unload cargo and detonate the charge."

Pausing, al-Nashiri, lifted an encrypted satellite phone to call a contact in the local Al Qaeda cell in Aden. The man answered on the third ring. Speaking an Arab dialect he said, "Aden Import Services."

"As-salam alaykum, do you have the materials I ordered last week?"

"Wa-Alaikum-Salaam, we are waiting for the payment to clear, and will have the items very soon."

Al-Nashiri suspected the necessary funds had not been received from their benefactor. He was a man of great patience but was determined to maintain the schedule for the purchase of the boat, explosives and other necessities. He would call Khallad to demand an answer.

TWENTY-FOUR

Tim sipped warm coffee from a Chicago Bears mug as Hugh rolled up to the console in a wheeled office chair. Speaking with a hint of Irish brogue Hugh smiled, "Tim, I know we have not yet had a chance to get properly acquainted, but Conrad has asked me to bring you into this op, and I need to leave for the airport very soon." Rising from his chair Hugh went on, "I want to show you something."

The two men walked out of the control room to the elevator at the end of the hall. Hugh opened the doors, stepped into the empty car, and motioned for Tim to follow. Hugh retrieved a key from his pocket and opened a panel in the elevator wall where Tim saw a keypad and a retinal scan port. Hugh went through the proper sequence and the elevator began to descend. When the doors opened, Hugh led Tim out of the elevator and through another door with another set of security devices. Hugh flipped a light switch immediately flooding the room in a harsh fluorescent light. Tim was immediately impressed. The walls were lined with handguns, long guns, automatic weapons, silencers, body armor, edged weapons, and other assorted deadly tools. Hugh walked a few feet to his left to a wooden work bench. He opened a wooden box resting at the far end of the work surface, reached into the container and brought out a small, black metallic, rectangular box no larger than a small tape recorder. The box was devoid of any labels or other markings. Hugh turned and tossed the container to Tim who caught it before it fell to the floor.

Tim looked at the object in his left hand. "What's this?"

"That little item is what you will deliver to the Ibiza airport and place into a compartment on the underside of a Boeing Business Jet. When you have placed the box into the aircraft, you will push a little switch that will mechanically arm the explosive device. That's your part of this operation."

Tim eyes widened, "Are there explosives in this right now?"

Hugh smiled, "Yes and no. The Semtex is in there, but no ignition device. All you have in your hand is an inert, oily slab of the favorite eastern European military grade explosive with some wires. The initiator has not been installed."

Tim stared at Hugh, "Where are the blasting caps?"

Hugh cocked his head slightly to the right, rolled his eyes and let out an audible sigh, "I have them safely stored in an underground concrete bunker near the beach."

Tim relaxed. "How will this be detonated?"

"I added a barometric pressure sensor to the initiator. When the device senses the proper barometric pressure, the device detonates. Are you familiar with this method?"

"Yes, I've seen several of these, and had training in making these types of devices. I've also seen the results of detonation. How will the blasting cap be placed?"

"You will open the box, insert the blasting cap, connect the wiring, close the box and press the power switch to activate the circuits. I have installed a small, fail-safe module that will not allow the detonator to ignite until the device is above ten thousand feet."

"Hugh, how does the blasting cap get to the final destination for insertion into the Semtex?"

Hugh looked at Tim with a quizzical expression on his face, "Tim, you carry it in an armored container on the airplane you will be taking to Ibiza. Don't worry, I've done this many times in the past and never had a problem."

Tim thought, *This is a new wrinkle, I just got here, and they expect me to go into the field?*

Hugh walked toward the door, motioned to Tim to follow, and moved briskly into the hallway. They reversed their route back to the control room.

TWENTY-FIVE

Orderly chaos greeted the two men when they walked into the control room. Hugh went directly to Ron, "Hey Ron, someone has forgotten to bring Tim up to speed on the Ibiza airport project. I just showed him the device, and he seems to be a little out of the loop. Can you get this straightened out? Thanks."

Hugh turned sharply toward the door and left Ron and Tim facing each other at Ron's console.

Ron sat in his chair and motioned Tim to sit on a nearby vacant stool. "Hugh got a little ahead of the timeline with this. I was about to tell you what we have planned, but he got to you first. No harm done. You needed to see the equipment anyway."

"So, Ron, what is the plan everyone seems to know about but me?"

Ron leaned back in his chair, "Here is the 'Cliff Notes' version. You will join the crew of our Gulfstream V business jet as the 'Relief Captain' for the 4,000-mile non-stop trip. You might occasionally ride the right seat since the flight should take about nine hours and the pilots will need to take a break from time to time. But don't worry, both pilots are rated Captains and Instructors. When the airplane lands, it will be directed to park on the Executive Terminal ramp.

Arrangements have been made with our local assets to park the Gulfstream next to the target Boeing. The Prince, Ibn Al-Wahidi, is scheduled to arrive about an hour before you. Spanish Customs, Immigration and Airport Police will not allow his security team to remain on the parking ramp with the aircraft. You, however, will remain with the Gulfstream and only be on the ground for two hours. During that time, the aircraft will be serviced, the crew will file a new flight plan and you will plant the explosive device. The crew will tell the ground personnel at the airport that your passengers changed their plans and will not be leaving for another week. That will cover your arrival and quick departure without passengers or cargo.

After the Prince and his men have departed the parking ramp, and Customs has inspected his airplane for contraband, you will have thirty minutes to place the device in the Boeing. We will provide you with a schematic of the Boeing with the specific fuselage panel designated to hide the explosives. Study the information so you can do it in the dark because that is exactly what you will be doing. You will have night-vision goggles and the necessary tools to remove and replace the small inspection panel. Any questions to this point?"

Tim rose from the stool and stretched. "No nothing right now, but I need to think about all this."

Ron nodded, "I know you have some questions. Take your time. You don't leave for a while.

TWENTY-SIX

The command center was awash in financial searches, asset inquiries and generally organized turmoil. About three hours later, Tim noticed Hugh was not at his station. Maybe he was at the gym, the armory or out for a run. When not in the control room, he was honing his professional skills. Hugh was a Field Operative, not a desk man.

Ingrid brought a flash drive to Ron and Tim. "Look at this. Hugh left it for us before he went to JFK airport two hours ago." Tim put the flash drive into a USB port, pressed a computer key and watched the screen come alive with an image of Hugh. He was wearing the traditional Yemeni 'zenneh', an ankle-length shirt, with a 'jambia', or dagger on his belt, and a navy blue, sport coat. His skin color appeared to be a few shades darker than yesterday. Hugh began to speak. "In accordance with the Op Plan, I am in transit to my meet with our man in Aden. I booked a flight on Emirates Airlines to Dubai, where one of our assets will provide a petroleum company aircraft to take me to a spot in the Empty Quarter of the Yemeni desert several hours north of Aden. I have a driver and truck arranged to take me to our location in the city. 'Auf wiedersehen,' Kurt."

Kurt strode into the Control Room like a man on a mission. "Events are moving more quickly than anticipated. Hence, Hugh goes to Aden. About an hour ago, Conrad shared a message from the directors. They have reason to believe that this planned attack in Yemen will greatly contribute to more destabilization in their portfolios and spheres of influence. They need to demonstrate their ability to control one of their rogue internal factions. Apparently, this faction is attempting to seize more control and power for their group. In other words, it is the start of a civil war within the directorate, and it must be crushed. Hugh will ensure favorable results for our position. Tim you, too, will provide an emphatic visual statement from our directors to these impudent upstarts."

Kurt checked his watch and continued, "As you already know, according to our sources Al-Nashiri seeks a dhow, the ordinary boat used for many purposes in the Arab world. We will provide the item through one of our assets. The competing faction boasts of its power to control or initiate actions beneficial to their positions, contrary to the covenants of the group. Our actions are intended to have a quieting and humiliating effect, causing the miscreants and their survivors to think twice about trying to undermine the directors. We need to maintain a close watch on movements of funds, personnel, and political influences during this critical time. We must also be prepared to act quickly on any instructions from the primary director concerning the termination of a member with extreme prejudice. Tim, Ron, please meet me in the library in an hour." Kurt turned on his heels, and quickly left the room. His appearance and demeanor gave the distinct impression of a well-oiled machine, a man accustomed to giving orders and having them obeyed without hesitation.

He had just demonstrated the nature of the Directorate. This group of directors combines quite an assembly of characters. Both sides of the law. No sides of the law, while simultaneously holding every position in the legal and ethical spectrum.

Tim paused for a few moments and considered the information he had just received. *I suppose one could argue that the best weapon against evil is the judicious use of evil and that betrayal could be an effective weapon. Once again, you need to intimately 'know' the enemy to be able to understand and defeat him. Seems like we have a high percentage of resident evil in this group. Managing this moral, ethical and psychological dilemma is the bailiwick for Ingrid, not me.*

TWENTY-SEVEN

Tim and Ron found the gleaming kitchen staffed by the resident chef and two young assistants. The chef spoke to them without turning, "What can I do for you gentlemen? If you are hungry, I have cold meats, salads, pastries, and the ingredients to make just about anything else."

They both decided on cold Italian sub sandwiches, macaroni salad and hot, Mexican, chocolate, cinnamon-spiced coffee. The cinnamon-chocolate addition to coffee made a near dessert, with the requisite sugar high, and caffeine jolt. Excellent choice to get through the afternoon doldrums. They took their meals and moved to a small table in a quiet nook at the far end of the kitchen.

Ron finished chewing a mouthful of macaroni salad while staring at an air handling duct near the ceiling and, much to the surprise of his lunch-mate, almost mechanically droned. "Ingrid is a widow. Her late husband was a CIA field operative who died from brain cancer a year after they were married. They never had children. She has a few personal issues, somewhat related to the job. When she started at the CIA, she was considered a rising star. Her work took her into many sensitive spheres, and that was when she discovered a very ugly truth. One day she stumbled across some highly classified documents. She discovered her parents did not die as the result of a common traffic accident. Her parents were murdered. They were a 'sleeper cell' of Stasi spies working in the United States. Someone discovered their true identities and arranged for the accident. I imagine you are wondering who directed their demise. The answer to that question has never been answered to her satisfaction. The United States Government was alleged to have been involved, but so was the KGB. Information indicates it was a double agent who saw an opportunity to please both bosses. With one act, he could collect double pay. It was an unsanctioned operation, and the double agent paid the ultimate price. His only problem was trying to collect twice. Public and classified records indicate he, too, was the victim of an auto accident. Poetic justice. However, Ingrid was never satisfied with that answer. She wants specifics, but that information probably lies within someone's head. The records are incomplete. Although two sides of the equation were happy with the results, the third side, the Stasi, had some issues. Today is the anniversary of the accident that killed her parents. Funny thing, she was recruited and hired by Kurt who worked for the same Stasi that cultivated the sleeper cell family. Our sources confirmed Ingrid was not a part of the game. She had no knowledge of her parents' life as spies. That has been verified through various methods of testing and screening before, during and after her recruitment. Her status was also verified by Kurt because he was the Stasi handler for that cell. Since there is proof that the directorate was not involved in their deaths, it is the perfect vehicle for her quest to find her 'holy grail,' the actual responsible person or persons. Hence, Kurt is very careful around her. No 'Lone Wolf' in this group. Just thought you should have this information. Let's get back to work."

TWENTY-EIGHT

The young prince, Ibn-al-Wahidi, sat quietly in front of a computer in his villa overlooking the Persian Gulf. He was scanning gold futures when a message alert jumped across the screen. The dispatch consisted of a telephone number followed by two five-character sequences. He immediately recognized the two sets of digital characters as a contact at Kennedy Airport. The young man owed a debt to the prince and his family, a debt that could never be paid in a single lifetime. Such was the way of his country and its rules. The young man worked for the national airline and was required to report certain information to the royal family. In this case, he thought he recognized a name on the passenger list of a flight to Dubai. A name that had been linked to a familiar United States Government agency. He thought, *I am not one hundred percent certain this is the same man on the list, but I must report it. If it is the same man, I will have done a service to my benefactor. If this is not the same man, I have acted with an over-abundance of caution, and will be safe.* He immediately picked up an encrypted, secure phone and dialed a phone number. "This is Ali at Kennedy" and proceeded to pass the information to his handler in New York. The information was sent further up the chain to the paranoid prince who believed this individual posed a threat to his position in the family and the Directorate. The passenger would be met at his destination, and silently dispatched to his ultimate fate, death.

Dark glasses concealed the intensely fierce eyes of the dark-skinned man. He had been waiting in the shadows of a bomb-damaged building near a commercial section of the wharf used by dozens of small costal freighters and numerous traditional wooden sailing ships known as "dhows". The combination of dead fish, exhaust fumes and cooking aromas filled his nostrils as he heard the clank of ship riggings, heavy cargo chains assorted machinery. Sweat ran down his back under the tan, traditional loose, long-sleeved, ankle-length garment worn by the men of Yemen. The garment cloaked not only the perspiration, but also the Russian, Makarov 9 mm pistol tucked in a pocket under his robe. He hated waiting, especially in the midday heat, but Sheikh Mansur, the Chechen, was a dedicated soldier. The small sixteen-meter ship with traditional, triangular sails known as "Lateens" neared the dock. Mansur thought to himself, *I hope "The Professor" knows what he is doing with this Shia boat owner. I have never trusted those people. If he fails us, he will pay the price. Allah may tolerate failure, but I don't."*

The dhow had moored at the dock when an Aden Harbor Police motor launch pulled alongside the dock. Mansur held his breath and moved his right hand onto the grip of the pistol through a slit in his outer garment. He could not hear what was being said, but he could see the men were comfortable with each other.

The uniformed policeman jumped onto the deck of the dhow and greeted the captain. "Cousin, how was your trip today? I imagine a visit from the Harbor Police is somewhat unwelcomed."

"You are always welcome on my vessel. We are family, and you know I have nothing to hide. I had a load of food for the Government dock. A few of the cases of canned meat fell during the operation, and I was able to retrieve them. If you wait a moment, I will share them with you." He disappeared into the cabin for a minute and returned with a case of meat. "They know me at the dock and usually leave my crew and me alone during the offloading. I only 'liberate' a very small amount. Much less than the dock workers, and no one asks questions. I go so often they don't even check my boat when I come and go."

The policeman smiled, "I know. Two of the dock workers are my brothers. They 'liberate' much more than you have. I will remind them you are our cousin. You shall receive even less scrutiny."

During the conversation between the captain and the policeman, the Al Qaeda operative inched closer to the boat and was able to overhear the conversation, especially the part about how the dhow was so familiar to the dock workers they paid no attention to it. He thought to himself, *This is better than we had hoped. This craft can get close to the US Navy ship, and no one will question its movements. I must tell the Professor about this. We must have this dhow.*

Once the Harbor Police launch was safely away from the dock and out of sight, Mansur moved into the open and walked toward the dhow. The captain had gone into the cabin and looked through a porthole at the man standing on the dock. The man was a stranger to the captain, but he knew the purpose. The captain took several photographs of the stranger to pass on to his relatives. These relatives had ties to several different groups with a common goal, to thwart Al Qaeda.

The stranger stopped at the edge of the dock at the dhow. "Hello! I need to speak to the captain! Is anyone there?"

The captain hesitated, then walked onto the deck at the gunwale. "I am the captain. What can I do for you?" The captain responded without the customary Islamic greeting.

Mansur immediately noted the failure to give the proper greeting, but let it pass without comment. "I wish to speak to you about purchasing your vessel. My associates tell me you want to sell this craft."

The captain stared blankly at the stranger, "Who told you that?"

Mansur had to think fast. This encounter was not going as smoothly as planned. This captain was a hard man, a careful man and possibly a dangerous man. "A friend. A friend who knows your cousin and is of his family."

The captain thought to himself, *I have taken this far enough. I have proven my point. Now I will begin the negotiation.* "Very well. Yes, I have spoken with your friend. Again, please tell me what you want."

Mansur wanted to relax, but he remained wary. "I wish to purchase this vessel at a fair price. My family owns several dhows in the Persian Gulf, and we want to expand our fleet. I am told this is a worthy vessel, that you intend to start another business and you are a fair man. I will offer you the market price."

The captain and Mansur both knew no one would make an offer on a boat they had never seen or had inspected.

Mansur also knew the captain was aware of who was actually offering to purchase the dhow. The captain stared off into the distance, "When will you need the boat?"

"Soon. I need to confirm the date with my family. Do you have a price?"

"I must think about this. It is time for prayers. After prayers I will consider my needs and arrive at what you would call a 'fair price' for this transaction. I understand the many issues associated with the sale of this craft, and the price will reflect my concerns with the issues." The captain needed time to report to his family and discuss the situation. Meet me here after evening prayers for my answer."

"I look forward to our meeting this evening."

The captain smiled, "As-Salamu Alaykum."

Mansur responded, "Wa-Alaikum-Salaam." Slightly confused by the unexpected Islamic phrase, he turned and disappeared into the maze of dilapidated buildings and dusty streets of the ancient port. A short distance later, he stopped at a bench under a solitary palm tree and removed a mobile phone from his pocket. After entering the number, he heard a voice at the other end of the line, "Yes? Go encrypted."

Mansur pressed several keys, heard a tone and said, "I have made contact. The transaction will be successful. I will call later tonight with more details." The call abruptly ended with a harsh click.

At about the same time Mansur was calling his contact, the captain was calling his family contact. "I just met with the Chechen. He will contact me again at the dock after evening prayers for my price and the schedule. We will speak later."

TWENTY-NINE

Eddie stood up at his computer station, "I have some 'com' traffic snagged by NSA and isolated by our program. Seems like our asset in Aden is in negotiations for the sale of his boat to some of Al-Nashiri's clan."

Kurt quietly said, "We have confirmed Hugh is aboard his Emirates Airlines flight to Dubai. The flight is scheduled for fourteen hours and twenty-five minutes, but it should arrive thirty minutes early. He arranged with one of our Directorate-friendly petroleum companies to provide a pilot and a helicopter. Now we wait. Hugh will ensure the boat used by Al-Qaeda will have a weakened hull below the water line. The combination of weakened wood joints, water pressure on the hull and the additional weight of several hundred pounds of explosives will send the craft to the bottom before it reaches the *USS Donovan*."

Tim mused, *An ingenious idea. Sink the boat before it can reach the target but do it in a manner that conceals the deliberate act of sabotage. No boat full of explosives, no explosion. The USS Donovan can complete the refueling operation, show the flag, and leave Aden before any problems. Directorate assets will ensure that the ship leaves port immediately after refueling on some pretense not known to the crew or Captain.* Tim relaxed in his chair, and silently wondered if it would work.

Eddie lounged in front of his computer in a near trance. He had been awake for nearly twenty hours in his constant battle with insomnia. The headphones covering his ears also concealed the heavy metal music coursing through his brain. Ingrid had been watching the young hacker all day. She was worried he was about to burn out from lack of sleep and sensory deprivation. Without warning, Eddie jumped out of his chair making a loud racket as his chair quickly rolled back and tipped over. "Kurt, I just intercepted a message from an Al Qaeda spy working as a ticket agent for Emirates Airlines at JFK.

He called someone to warn of a US Intelligence asset flying from New York to Dubai. It sounds like they are tracking Hugh!"

Ingrid calmly walked to Eddie, "Eddie, let me hear what you have." She was worried the young man had hallucinated. When he blankly stared at her, she softly touched his arm, "Eddie. I would like to hear the recording."

Breaking out of his daze, his intense eyes blazed, then relaxed. A few keystrokes later he called over his shoulder to Ingrid, I sent the recording to your computer. I need to call Kurt."

Kurt grimly walked to Eddie's computer station. "What do you have for me?"

"This phone call was captured by the electronic eavesdropping system at NSA. Our system intercepted and sent it to us. It will come up on the speaker in a second."

The tentative, mousy, male voice came weakly through the speakers, "This is Ali at Kennedy, a single, male traveler to Dubai is booked on the next flight. His name is exactly the same as an alias used by an American CIA agent. He is using the name, S. O'Farrell. I did not see him check-in, but he has been cleared for departure by Immigration." The nearly panicked airline employee ended the call with a click.

Kurt frowned, the message had been unclear, and lacked details. "The young caller is certainly not a professional asset. The information is nearly unusable, but never-the-less we need to advise Hugh of this situation. Eddie, send him a message when he lands. He is authorized to use any necessary measures. Ingrid, Tim what do you propose for our next step?"

Ingrid knew this question was not for her, but to test Tim. She leaned forward in her chair, "Tim, do you have any ideas?"

"Have we identified this airline employee? If not, then that is our first step. We then determine who he called and move up the chain. We monitor the communications of every individual in the chain to identify the network and expand our monitoring activities as you would in any complex investigation. We only monitor communications and other activities such as travel, finances and political and personal links. They are more useful as sources of information rather than targets at this time."

Kurt turned his expressionless face toward Ingrid, "Do you have comments, additions or adjustments?"

She shook her head. "No, not at this time. The actions seem reasonable and prudent."

Kurt nodded to no one in particular, "Good. Then you will coordinate with Eddie and Ingrid to perform the tasks you have outlined. I will be in Conrad's office if you require me."

Eddie and Ingrid turned their gaze to Tim. Eddie let out a little laugh, "Well, Tim, how did you like that little test? Don't worry, in a few years these little games will only occur very rarely."

Ingrid chided the young geek, "Eddie you know he never stops testing you."

"That's because he likes me more than you."

THIRTY

Seven minutes after the young Emirates Airlines employee had finished his call to his handler, the uncle received a telephone call on one of his encoded private lines. The British accent came through clearly as the voice warned that someone had probably penetrated their group or their communications. An infidel was coming to the Dubai Airport and the group needed to neutralize the threat. The uncle sat on a bench near the entrance to a mosque. He preferred the mosque for contemplation of many things, including his interactions with the prince. He knew this mosque contained no electronic monitoring devices because his brother, the Imam, had one of his cousins perform a "sweep" several times each day. The old man thought, *This, is an issue for the prince. I know what he will do, but I do not want this to come back to me. I must maintain my neutral appearance.* The old man moved from the bench to a secluded side room where he removed his cell phone from his pocket and dialed the prince on a secure line. The phone rang but went unanswered. *That fool must be engaged with some young thing or is involved in ingesting chemicals.* The man was nearly through the door when his phone chirped the code assigned to the prince. With a barely perceptible contempt, the uncle said, "Thank you for returning the call so promptly. Within the last five minutes I received a call from one of our friends at Interpol. It appears that we have an intruder in our midst scheduled to arrive at the Dubai airport from JFK in a few hours. This individual is an employee of our friends at Langley. The CIA must have some interest in our activities beyond the regular issues. What shall we do about this?"

Without hesitation, the prince spat out, "Kill him at the airport. Call the Chechen, he will know what to do." The line went dead.

The old man looked at his phone and said out loud to himself, "That fool only knows brutality and savagery. One day, very soon, he will make a mistake. I only hope I am not caught up in the disaster as collateral damage."

Two hours before Hugh was scheduled to arrive at the Dubai International Airport, a young Saudi man walked slowly through the concourse. He had just come in on a flight from Paris placing him in the throngs of arriving passengers from around the world moving to the Customs and Immigration Arrivals Hall. He slipped away from the stream of humanity at the "Duty Free" shops on the upper level to avoid the escalators delivering the arriving masses down to the main floor. No one paid any attention to the young, very slight, less than average height man with deep set, dark piercing eyes. If his blemished, nearly effeminate face had not been partially masked by the scraggly attempt at a beard, he could have passed as a young girl. His traditional Arab headdress and robe with slits allowing access to his western clothing worn under the robe completed his non-descript appearance at an Arab international airport. The stainless-steel mechanical pencil in his shirt pocket appeared to be a common accessory for most any traveler, and he was ready to use it.

Ready for the infidel who had defiled the lives of his maternal relatives, their heritage and Allah, the young Arab man had the duty and honor to remove this filth from the face of the earth. If he could be martyred in this effort, it would be a welcomed gift. So, he waited in anticipation of thrusting the innocuous device into the base of the brain of this Infidel, this Hugh O'Farrell. Remembering the emergency telephone call, he replayed the conversation in his mind for the umpteenth time, *This is Kallad, you will immediately go to the Emirates ticket counter at De Gaulle Airport. Your ticket to Dubai will be waiting for you. Upon arriving at Dubai, you will wait on the upper level by the Duty-Free shops for the Infidel known as Hugh O'Farrel. Use the mechanical pencil provided to you. This man must not leave the airport alive. Follow him through Immigration and Customs. When in the main terminal, and among the throngs, use the device. Your target will be the only middle-aged Westerner on the Emirates flight from New York arriving twenty minutes after you land. He is balding and will be wearing a brown suit. Contact your handler after you have completed your task. May Allah be with you.* The line went dead. The young Arab, however, had been given some misinformation. Accurately reported, O'Farrel was on the flight, but the manifest listed an S. O'Farrell, not Hugh Farrell. Master S. O'Farrel was a three-month old baby travelling with the Jamieson's, his middle-aged aunt and uncle. The young man was not aware of his problem. He only knew that an Infidel named Hugh O'Farrell must be killed. He did not know why, nor did he care. His duty was to follow orders from his brothers in Allah.

THIRTY-ONE

Tim was tired and began nodding when his brain was jarred back into the "now" of the control room. Ingrid stood up from her chair at her array of monitors, "I believe we have an escalating situation in Dubai. Voice and text intercepts identified by our systems indicate we have a security breach in our Yemen op. It seems someone knows of an Irishman coming into Dubai and presumes it is one of our assets or a CIA asset. They don't know any more but are actively trying to get the information to pass it on to an operative flying from Paris to Dubai to terminate the Irishman. They believe the man known to them as "O'Farrell" is coming in on our Emirates Airlines flight from JFK. The manifest has an S. O'Farrell, but he is a three-month old baby. They must have confused our Hugh with this unsuspecting non-combatant."

Kurt had entered the room just as Ingrid started speaking and heard the entire report. "Ingrid, do we have a lock on the source of the breach?"

Ingrid continued to examine her screen. "The information is still being massaged, but the original source seems to be through a low-level Emirates Airlines employee at JFK, then eventually to one of our directors, Ibn Al-Wahidi. We've had some troubling traffic from him in the past, so specific 'traps' were included his personal communications system. The directors have had reservations about him for some time now and appear to be justified."

Kurt looked troubled. "I need to speak with Conrad. Ingrid, are you certain of the original source?"

"Yes. This has been vetted using five independent sources that have been accurate in the past over ten times. Nothing is ever positive, but this information has the highest level of confidence."

"This is disturbing, but not surprising. This director has been compartmentalized for some time now. Excellent work, Ingrid. Please keep me apprised as the situation progresses." Kurt disappeared into the hallway leading to Conrad.

Tim lounged at his console watching and listening as Emirates Airlines began its descent into the Dubai Airport.

Kurt had asked Tim to notify him when the airliner began its initial descent. Watching radar screen depictions provided by Eddie, "The Hacker", and listening to the radio traffic, he heard when the flight was cleared to descend and contact Dubai Approach. He notified Kurt on the internal communications network and gave him the status.

THIRTY-TWO

The landing and taxi to the gate were normal. Hugh planned to walk off the plane in his Arab garb appearing to all the world as a local traveler returning home.

Inside the terminal, the hands of the solid gold Rolex clock on the terminal wall displayed nine o'clock in the morning. The young Arab assassin anxiously waited outside the entry to a gold merchant at the end of the concourse. From his vantage point, the young Arab could watch the schedule board listing all arriving flights and the entrance to Customs and Passport Control. He was looking for the Irishman when he saw a bald, European man in a brown suit carrying a bundle. This was the only person fitting the nearly non-existent description. The young Arab decided he would follow him through Passport Control and Customs, kill him quietly as the throngs of passengers moved into the main terminal, then walk out of the building into the masses of Dubai and the endless desert.

A tall, young, blonde, Croatian woman stood behind one of the jewelry counters near the rear of the store eyeing the young Arab. The traveler appeared to be sweating heavily causing the clerk to consider whether the young man might be ill. She had seen thousands of people from third world countries as they passed her door in their relentless progress toward the giant Arrivals Hall. Some of them would be detained by Health Officials if they presented a potential health threat. She reached into the jacket pocket where she kept a silent alarm panic button if she needed the police. She did not want anything to mar her perfect record on the job, especially any contact with someone who might have a rare, contagious disease. She fingered the small plastic and metal transmitter trying to decide on her next move when the young man moved quickly to the edge of the throng of humanity moving like molten lava through the concourse.

Hugh powered his cell phone and watched the screen come alive as he waited for the aircraft door to open. The phone was equipped with a special feature that gave a pulsing icon when a "Flash" message had been received. "Flash" was the directorate's equivalent of a 911 call. When Hugh saw the pulsing icon, he turned the phone to his face so the sensor could interrogate the pupil of his right eye. After the computer confirmed his identity, he entered his personal digital code, and placed the phone to his ear. The message from Ingrid was succinct. "Possible compromise. Young Arab assassin waiting inside terminal to execute you. Believes you to be Hugh O'Farrell, an Irish national. Leak in the arrangements. Single director compromised op. Managing here. Proceed with caution." He prepared himself for the next segment of the mission. In his current disguise, he would not be mistaken for an Irish national, but he would need to quickly and quietly, terminate this threat. He sent a brief message to the control room. "Arrived. Message received." He closed his phone, hurried into the terminal, and proceeded to the Customs and Immigration Arrivals Hall.

THIRTY-THREE

The young Arab was obvious to Hugh. He watched the assassin searching the faces of the crowd as it moved into the Customs and Immigration Arrival Hall, his gaze intently studying each European face. His fixed examination of every Infidel was so rigid that an Israeli tank could have rolled past the young man without notice. Hugh, the young Arab, and the crowds continued toward Passport Control. All Europeans were processed at passport gates separate from the general masses and the residents of Dubai. Carrying a United Arab Emirates passport, Hugh quickly cleared Immigration without waiting more than a few seconds for a bored Immigration Official to stamp his documents. Hugh moved toward the exit keeping the assassin in his periphery, blended into the crowd, and moved into a doorway near the entry to Baggage Claim and Customs. He watched a bald man in a brown suit carrying a baby trying to navigate the crushing crowd when the assassin came into view, a few steps behind his unsuspecting prey. The young Arab moved closer to his target. Fixed pupils, face drained of all color, the young assassin acted like a man on a mission. Hugh readied his own mechanical pencil. The lead was a needle, the ink was a "witches brew" of potassium cyanide, and an untraceable additive. A yellow liquid designed to stop the heart within seconds, impersonating a heart attack. He loved 'Designer Drugs." Hugh saw the Arab closing in on the man and baby with more intensity and tunnel vision. The young Arab never saw Hugh coming out of the doorway to join the knot of travelers. Hugh slipped up beside him and put his right arm around the shoulders of the young Arab as if they were old friends. The arm was intended to hold and control the target, not an embrace. As the young man, startled and confused, looked to his left, Hugh deftly slid the needle into the side of the neck at the carotid artery. Hugh held the dead man for several moments to ensure the chemicals had sufficient time to work. He felt the muscles in the body begin to slacken, released his hold on the late assassin, and quickly merged with the mass of humanity moving into the main terminal. Noise and commotion erupted where the body of the young man had fallen. Hugh walked calmly through the terminal exit inspecting faces in the crowd for any hint of problems. No one seemed to notice him. He was just an Arab traveler coming out of the terminal. Outside, the sky was clear, the day was warm, and the heavy traffic congestion was exactly what Hugh needed.

THIRTY-FOUR

Hugh took the tram to long term parking and hunted for his ride. After ten minutes he opened the door to his new transportation, a silver, Mercedes S450 sedan. The parking lot entry ticket lay on the seat. The car had come into the lot about two weeks ago and was covered with the usual layer of desert. Many Europeans came to work the oil fields and construction sites in the Emirates. When they either got tired of Dubai, or lost their jobs, they simply drove to the airport, parked their car, and took the next airplane home. Sometimes, they left the door unlocked with the keys in the ignition. This owner was never returning to Dubai, so he just walked away from everything associated with his life in this desert oasis. Hugh started the engine and found the fuel gauge at the half-full mark. Or was it half empty?

He drove the silver Benz out of the parking lot with no problem since the owner had an unexpired long-term parking pass. The highway took him southwest to the Port of Jebel, where he had arranged to meet a helicopter leased by a Norwegian oil company. Ten o'clock in the morning and he had already dispatched one of the "competition."

The Russian-built Mi-26 helicopter should be waiting for him at a helipad located near the oil company offices. The pilot believed he would be delivering a corporate, bigwig to a remote exploration site east of the city of Sharurah, Yemen, at the south end of the Empty Quarter. A seven-hundred-mile trip faced the Mi-26, but it was rated to go eleven hundred miles on a full internal load of fuel. The pilot could deliver his cargo non-stop, go to the Sharurah airport, refuel and leave, or spend the night.

About thirty minutes later, Hugh arrived at the oil company compound. He parked the car, removed his Arab garb, and became Hugh the Irish petroleum engineer. He left the car parked in a visitor spot, took his leather overnight bag containing his Arab costume and began the next phase of his operation.

In a dusty part of Aden, Yemen, the Chechen, Khallal, sat on a bench in the sparsely populated mosque waiting for the phone call. His contact in Dubai should have called him by now with the news that the bald westerner was dead, but only silence surrounded him. He waited a few more minutes then called the contact. No formalities. No Islamic greeting. Quietly, with a poorly controlled intensity, "What the hell has happened? There has been enough time for the task to be accomplished."

The meek voice responded, "Our man failed. He is dead. Our people do not know what happened other than he was killed by lethal injection in the terminal among the crowd of travelers between Immigration and Customs. I have no further information."

"What about the target?"

More hesitation, "I am afraid we had inaccurate information. Our people at the airline discovered the intended target is a baby, not the Directorate or CIA operative. We are trying to confirm the original information but have had no luck.:

The Chechen paused, then quietly said, "We must do better next time," then ended the call. He thought to himself. *Something is wrong. I can feel it. We are too near the execution date for the bombing. I must speak to more sources. Events are occurring of which we have no knowledge. It is nearly time for prayers. I shall remain and reflect. Allah will show me the way. Praise Allah.*

A short walk past two rows of metal buildings brought Hugh to the helicopter pad. Standing on the pad, he could see the pilot inside the office relaxing in a leather lounge chair, drinking a coke. Hugh waited a few seconds by the huge helicopter before the senior pilot ambled out into the morning sun. Although they had never met, Hugh recognized the type. Ten years past his prime, tired eyes, thin frame and a graying crew cut from the 1960's military. Probably a former Marine. There are no "ex-Marines", only "ex-wives" according to several of his" Yank" friends who had been Marines. This kind of guy can usually fly the pants off younger guys using skill, cunning and the occasional unapproved maneuver. Perfect for the task today.

The pilot came within a few feet of Hugh, scanned him and pronounced, "You must be my passenger, but you sure as hell don't look like an oil geek. Not my business, though. Cal Williams is the name. I've been here in the desert too long, but now I call it home. Ready?"

Hugh thought, *He never asked my name. Good guy. Appears very capable, down to the pistol in a soft holster concealed inside his jacket beneath his left arm. Probably works under sensitive conditions. Probably has been doing this type work for quite a while.*

"Well, Mr. Oil Field Engineer, let's go. This trip will take a few hours." Williams slid into his seat and a few seconds after the necessary radio calls to air traffic control they were off the ground turning south into the desert. They flew in silence south into the vast Arabian Peninsula and began their four-hour trip toward the thousands of square miles of stark desert known as the Empty Quarter. Cal motioned to a thermos of coffee, American coffee, hot and black. Hugh lifted himself out of the seat looked on a shelf at the rear of the giant cockpit and found a dozen Styrofoam coffee cups. He poured two cups about half full and handed one to Cal who nodded and continued to scan the sky in front of the rotary wing aircraft. Not much to see. A pale blue sky with wisps of high cirrus clouds meeting multi-colored sand at the horizon filled the large windscreen. Hugh looked around the cockpit, realized he was in the largest helicopter built by man and wondered why this particular machine had been provided. In a few minutes he got his answer.

Cal looked at him and pronounced in a short, clipped military fashion, "Not only did your company request this mode of transportation they also paid for the truck secured in the cargo compartment under the tarp. The Toyota company makes a fine vehicle, especially for desert rats."

Hugh had not made these arrangements. Although his outward appearance remained rigid, his guts were in turmoil. *Cal must know more than needed. Why? Why break the "need-to-know" protocols?*

Cal gave a sidelong glance across the cockpit, "Confused? I would be if I were you. Relax. Kurt and I go back a long way. We were friendly adversaries in the bad old days. As you know, he was Stasi, and I was on our side, whatever side that may be. He and I worked the Russians, not each other. We needed blinders to do our jobs, and we had them on through nearly everything. Of course, we could only go so far since we didn't trust each other, but it did go far enough to keep both of us alive on more than one occasion. Our Russian friends never knew, and rightly so. Neither the Stasi nor our side really knew about our personal arrangement. I suppose I could have lost my retirement and freedom if the bureaucrats ever realized what we did, although I never really got my retirement. I left when I saw the time was right, and other opportunities became realized."

"So, who is your employer? The oil company?"

Cal squinted through his aviator sunglasses at the desert in front of them, "Oil company? I only borrow their toys when necessary. This is in scheduled maintenance on a helicopter that never existed. It has been 'off the books' for the past twelve years. The oil company should never know about our trip and this craft will be back in Iraq after the mechanics finish their work. Kurt called me and went through the story of your current op. I had some time, so I volunteered to be your sidekick, Lone Ranger." Cal sighed, "Kurt and I have worked together over the past few years. He asked me to join the group more than once, but I like my mundane existence, so I declined. He still calls when he needs me to bail his sorry Teutonic ass out of a problem. So here we are in a stolen, pardon, 'liberated' helicopter, the largest helicopter in production. The FAA claims this has a crew of five, but the oil company has done some modifications so just one pilot can take care of all operations. The FAA doesn't have jurisdiction outside the US."

Hugh was pissed. He wasn't pissed because Kurt had introduced someone else into the mix. He was upset because Kurt had failed to give him a "heads up" call. Well, no time for personal issues. The mission came first, and Kurt was only helping. Back to work.

"Cal, it sounds like you will not be flying this thing back north."

"Kurt asked me to join you on your trip to Aden and provide any help you might need." Obviously, he knew the implications of his presence. He knew Hugh had no knowledge, nor had given any approval. A very toxic mix for a field op. Cal knew Kurt should have told Hugh, but Cal was being paid to do a job, not to think about family squabbles.

Hugh scanned the horizon with laser beams instead of his eyes. The uneasy silence was broken when Hugh turned to Cal who was fiddling with a radio. "Not your fault, Cal. My issue is with Kurt. But if he brought you on board, he must have a damn good reason. Seems like two professionals thrown into a situation not of their making. Standard day."

"When we land, I'll get the truck out of storage back there. What is your plan after we land?"

Hugh thought for a moment, "I plan to stay in these western clothes until I get on the road into the desert, then change into my Arab persona. When I get to Aden, I'll clear the safe house, meet my contact, and start the next phase. Of course, Kurt will get an update." He let a darkness cross his face for just an instant as he turned away from Cal, but just slow enough for his new partner to get a glimpse.

THIRTY-FIVE

The evening sun began to fade into a dull orange glow near the horizon when Cal flew over the landing site to check winds and conditions. He turned toward Hugh, "Looks okay, but you never know what to expect in this god-forsaken corner of the world. Bandits, terrorists, and desert crazies all inhabit this empty, desolate piece of dirt."

They both looked at the compound with experienced eyes and senses. Nothing seemed out of the ordinary. Cal made a wide turn into the hot, sand-laden wind of the Arabian Desert. When Cal eased the helicopter to the hot desert floor, the aging craft lurched and vibrated from the turbulence as dust swirled around their landing zone, briefly engulfing the craft.

When the blades silently slowed to a stop, Cal quickly unbuckled the seat harness, eased out of the seat and moved to the rear door of the machine. He reached for some electric control switches and the rear door opened to a dull brown and bright blue scene.

Cal and Hugh jumped off the ramp and stood like statues on the sand next to the open rear cargo door. The landing zone appeared to be secure. No vehicles, no people, no sounds other than the whine of desert winds. Cal came up behind Hugh with his right hand wrapped around the pistol grip of a Czech CZW9, machine gun. Cal raised the barrel of the weapon to aim it directly at a point just to the right of Hugh's ear. A burst of flame and metal screamed past Hugh to find the center mass of a burqa-clad human shape. Hugh turned, dropped, and rolled to face Cal. Again, silence except for the wind. Cal lowered his weapon and quickly moved to the heap of humanity and cloth laying on the sand. He checked the body, pulled back the traditional female outer garment to reveal the remains of a bearded man still clutching a Russian, AK-74 Assault Rifle.

Hugh rose from his defensive stance, walked to Cal, looked at the body and said, "What the hell just happened?!?"

Cal looked up from the body, scratched his head, and softly said to no one in particular, "Habib, I owe you again." He turned to Hugh with a grim expression etched into his face, "My friend, Habib, called on our secure Satellite Phone just before you arrived at the heliport up north. His cousin hinted that we might have a reception committee. This is a closed facility. No one has been here for over three months. When Habib alerted me, I called Kurt. He had Ingrid review satellite images of this place and discovered recent activity. People and trucks were here early this morning. Before that, nothing. Habib was at a local truck stop and overheard one of the drivers who had delivered stolen oil field explosives to this site. He and his two brothers were going to grab the load. This crew has been pulling this kind of job for over a month. This time they picked the wrong load. They were only common thieves, and nothing else."

Puzzled, Hugh looked down at the solitary body. "I thought you said he had two brothers in this deal."

Appearing from the brown desert canvas behind a brick hut, Habib smiled sheepishly, "Mr. Hugh, the other two are behind that building. You did not hear my pistol." He reached into the folds of his traditional Yemeni robe and retrieved the Italian Beretta Model 71 pistol with silencer, the favorite assassin weapon of the Israeli Mossad.

Hugh was overwhelmed by the information he just got from Cal and silently wondered, *If Cal was so connected with Kurt, why had Hugh never heard of him? How did Cal know Ingrid? What was happening? Surprisingly, he didn't question the presence of the three bandits who were ready to kill him.*

His thought processes were interrupted when Cal smiled and openly opined, "Questions? Confusion? A little anger, feeling of insecurity in a supposedly controlled environment?"

Hugh turned and nodded. His expression hardened, accompanied by a flash of anger in his eyes. "You bet your ass I'm pissed." Hugh spit out the words between clenched teeth. "This op has been a 'goat rope' ever since I got to Dubai, and apparently, it started before I arrived."

Cal held up his hands in submission and took two steps back. "The Directorate team intercepted voice and data traffic after you were airborne from New York and had no way to get the info to you. Seems like one of the directors has an agenda contrary to the common good of the group. They ordered Kurt and the team to maintain surveillance on the renegade director's communications. The old men never trusted the young upstart but let him join the Directorate at the request of one of the founding families. As you can imagine, much embarrassment will be heaped upon the shoulders of that old family. The problem director has a scheme in which he and his small group of trusted family members will replace the 'old guard' with their people. The usurper doesn't trust, or like, Infidels. The actions of this rebellious young director are intended to embarrass the established old families and demonstrate the power and reach of this new, young director in the name of Allah and the almighty dollar. Kurt brought me into this op to help you on the ground, and ensure you get whatever assets you need. Your sources for equipment may have been compromised. That's the reason I brought the Toyota. The details of the plan have not changed. Sabotage the Al Qaeda boat, foil the attack, and ride off into the sunset before they know what happened."

Hugh took a few seconds to process the new information. "Well then, let's get started. Has my boat source changed?"

Cal studied a spent bullet cartridge half-buried in the sand for a moment. "No."

Without pause, he changed the subject back to the operation. "Our local asset has arranged for the use of a boat from a known thief and smuggler. That individual most likely will not be able to pursue his chosen career for more than a few days from now if our mission is successful. Our 'Freedom Fighter' friends have little tolerance for failure, and his boat will fail."

Cal had spoken as if he were conducting the morning intelligence briefing for the President and his staff. No emotion, just words. They waited in silence for a few minutes while the winds began covering the remains of the intruders with the relentless desert sand. The ever-changing landscape of the desert created constant change without change. That is the character of this part of the world. He finished removing the truck from the helicopter and preparing the craft for its return to Iraq by Habib.

"Well, Mister Oil Engineer, it's time for us to go to the city. I continue to be an oil company field worker going to the big city for a good time."

THIRTY-SIX

Al-Nashiri sipped tea as he sat at a table in an interior room of a house in a remote rural Pakistan village near the Afgan border. Engrossed in thought while considering his next attack he ignored the other two men quietly studying maps of the area surrounding one of the major United States military bases in central Afghanistan. They compared satellite images and photos taken by other Al Qaeda operatives on and near the base with their personal knowledge and observations gathered over the past months. Sounds from a minor commotion in one of the outer rooms slipped into the room annoying AL-Nashiri. His senses warned him as he reached for the assault rifle resting on the table. One of his trusted lieutenants rushed into the room, "Our man at the Dubai airport has been murdered! The dead man is the one sent to kill the American CIA Agent O'Farrell. Our man who arranged for the assassination heard from his network at the airport. The intended target, the American, has disappeared. We know he arrived, but the man slipped through our grasp."

Al Nashiri moved his hand from the assault rifle, rubbed the back of his neck then looked directly at his lieutenant, "We do not know why this American came to Dubai or where he is now. We do not know anything other than an American CIA operative has arrived at Dubai. What are your concerns?"

"Is it possible they know about our plans for the Yemen harbor?"

"Anything is possible, but we have no information they are aware of our operation. Have our people find this man and report to me as soon as you have completed the task. Thank you for your concern, but do not give the Americans too much credit."

The Chechen, seated at a table in a plain brick building on the outskirts of Djibouti, tightly squeezed his cell phone, "The American CIA Agent has killed our assassin at the Dubai airport."

The prince demanded, "And how do you know that? Were you there at the airport?"

"Our man is dead. He was to intercept and kill the American. Who else would have done that? Our man was poisoned with a jab into the carotid artery. Do you realize how difficult that tactic would be in a crowded airport? That, is an expert at work, not the hand of God or some amateur."

"I suppose you are correct, but how did the American know he was a target, and how did he come to have that specific tool with him?"

"We have a leak in our organization! That is how, and the leak is not from my people. You have a problem. You are too cozy with the Americans."

The lack of respect from this goat herder was beginning to push to the surface as the prince became furious. "If you value your life, you will remember who you are speaking to. I am not one of your dirt farmers."

The Chechen, realizing he may be too close to the brink, slowed his speech and lowered his tone, "We are all in this together for the glory of Allah. What is done, is done, and we need to move on. I will check my organization for leaks or compromises."

"And I shall do the same. Is your timeline for Aden still intact? Do you require anything from me?"

"All is well and on schedule."

They ended the call with the traditional farewells.

The Chechen quickly dialed another number. The first ring had barely ended when a soft female voice answered, "Hello?"

"Have you heard of the incident at the Dubai airport?"

"Yes. We have contacted our people at the airline and at the airport. Our man was killed without any attempt at defense. Surveillance cameras at the airport terminal captured the entire event. His attacker knew we were waiting for him but struck before our man could act. The murder was very quiet, clean and professional. The individual who killed our man was wearing traditional clothing and disappeared into the crowd. We lost him somewhere inside the terminal. The police are reviewing all video outside the terminal but have no new information. Our people have the body. They will ensure a false identification in case infidels attempt to tie this to us."

The Chechen ended the call and thought, *Something is wrong. I can feel it. I must go to Aden to personally control this.* His paranoia had served him well in the past. He learned to have a healthy respect for self-doubt. He called to one of his subordinates in the next room, "I need to go to Aden, immediately." Within the hour, the Chechen was on a forty-two-foot, Cigarette boat painted flat gray.

The captain estimated he would arrive at their destination in less than three hours. A flat sea and calm winds would provide the perfect conditions.

THIRTY-SEVEN

The Toyota rolled south on the smooth, paved road to Aden, and the next chapter in this saga. The dangerous port city lay at the end of three hundred miles of desert passing scrub trees, grasses, rivers, mountains, and endless miles of sand and sky. The men took turns driving, only stopping at infrequent population centers when the body or the fuel gauge demanded attention. No one noticed the two men in an oil company truck. Many similar men were driving similar vehicles. Toyota seemed to be the favorite, although some Mercedes, and the occasional Fuso Japanese truck also joined the sparse parade.

The sun sets quickly in the desert. The subtle glow of lights on the horizon rapidly became a blanket of twinkling diamonds belying the drab face of the city. Both men were lost in thought as they moved closer to the end game. They entered the outskirts of the port city of Aden, eerily cloaked in silence, as they drove along the coast to a small lane tucked between two high concrete walls. The Toyota barely squeezed through the portal onto an ancient stone lane and continued until they came to a large wooden and steel-clad gate set into a seven-foot-high stone wall. No visible identifying marks or numbers, but Hugh knew exactly where he was. He was an infrequent visitor to the house of his uncle, Mustafa al

Shaqqaf, and only appeared at the heavy doors when he faced challenges no one else could reconcile. Mustafa was more than just his uncle. He was a protector, and an asset for the Directorate.

The Toyota eased to a silent stop. No sounds except for shorebirds lazily floating overhead, asking, *"Who was this interloper?"* Without notice, the heavy gate quietly swung open. No sound other than a quietly whirring electric motor somewhere behind the wall. Cal drove into the yard. Another bleak wall with a simple wooden door stared back at them. Nothing fancy or ornate, just a solid door weathered gray by the sun, wind, salt air and time. The scene reminded Hugh of a "Sallyport" entrance to a prison. The second door cannot open until the first door is closed and locked. They slipped from their seats, stretched, and moved toward the second door. Once inside, they found themselves in a lush garden. They elegant figure of a man wearing a welcoming smile and traditional garb, greeted the men. A stately figure that at once demanded respect but radiated kindness at the edges. Hugh knew very well that this civilized figure had brutally killed and maimed many men, but this was a moment for devoted family members to reunite and restore old bonds.

They exchanged hugs and traditional greetings, "My Nephew, As-Salamu Alaykum."

"My Uncle, Wa-Alaikum-Salaam."

"Your Mother's sister has been saving a place for you at our table for some time and I am blessed to have you in my home. But forgive me, I have not properly greeted our other guest. As-Salamu Alaykum my friend."

"Wa-Alaikum-Salaam. I am Cal, a friend and associate of young Hugh, and am honored to be in your house."

"Kurt has spoken of you and your part in this endeavor facing us. Please come inside where we can relax with some refreshment, and Hugh can tell me of his courageous exploits and conquests. His conquests, however, cannot be recounted until his aunt is sufficiently hidden in another room, although I know she spies on us like the stars in the night air. I believe she, too, twinkles when the accounts of certain exploits become stimulating, although I would be severely chastised if she were to know of my suspicions."

They removed their dirty boots, donned soft slippers and walked through a short entry corridor adorned with tapestry and desert flora providing a world of color and sweet fragrances. The hallway ended at an interior courtyard covered with a glass roof. Diffused light delicately played on beautiful mosaics, verdant plants, and a softly sparkling fountain.

The calm of the moment was gently disturbed by the smooth, serene voice of the woman standing between luxuriant ferns guarding either side of a doorway leading to the rest of the house. They exchanged greetings and warm hugs, "Hugh, I hope your journey has gone well, and your life's journey pleases Allah."

"My dear Aunt, my journey is complete now that I am in your household again." He turned toward Cal and gestured, "My dear Aunt, this is a trusted friend, Cal. He will help us during the next phase of our journey."

She spoke to Cal, "As-Salamu Alaykum."

He responded, "As-Salamu Alaykum."

Mustafa looked at his wife. "My dear, we men have some private things to discuss. Would you give us a few minutes? We shall not require much time."

She looked at Mustafa with a stern face, but a sparkle in her eyes and said, "We shall see. I must oversee the preparation of food and drink, so I leave you to your uncle and his stories. I have heard the same lies too many times, and they become more outlandish with each telling."

In the tradition of many cultures, the three men spoke of family, and travels, and stories of the past, but no business. According to custom, business could wait for pleasantries, food, and drink to be completed. Serious discussion would come soon enough.

THIRTY-EIGHT

After they had eaten, spoken of mutual histories, the time had come for the necessary discussion. Mustafa led the group to an ancient door equipped with a modern electronic lock. He moved a tapestry to the side of the door frame revealing a fingerprint scanner, cypher lock and a biometric retinal scanner set into the wall. Not your average tenth century Moorish entry system. He went through the necessary steps, opened the door, then turned and smiled at Hugh and Cal. "I work with Kurt from time to time. He insisted upon these measures. They are equal to the CIA Security Directive, DCID9, incorporating specific electronic security requirements known as 'Tempest.' Please, enter my humble workshop."

Once inside, Cal looked around the room. He knew Mustafa was certainly a distinguished gentleman of adequate means, but this was something else. The room was more like the office of the character "Q" from James Bond, or a mad scientist. Several computers, a laser, a gas chromatograph, a chemical fume hood, various glass vials and beakers, a gun rack, an encrypted telephone, and countless other big boy toys were all neatly placed around the room. *Nice old man, my ass! This was a wizard's room. A wizard of warfare, secrecy, violence, and subversion.* Mustafa blandly watched Cal as he took in the display.

Hugh broke the silence with, "Cal, what do think? Not bad for a retired gentleman living on a backwater street, in the middle of one of the most dangerous places in the world."

Mustafa stood back with the look of a proud parent after his son perfectly played *Claire de Lune* at his music school recital. "I must admit, this is my 'man cave,' and refuge from my wife. This room is secure, so I can say many things without the horrible repercussions of a displeased wife, let alone our friends at the Directorate. In other words, this room is constructed to stop electromagnet signals, sounds or mechanical vibrations from leaving the premises." Even his demeanor had changed when the electronic lock clicked, and the door to this little corner of hell opened. This was definitely not a UNESCO site for saving humanity through peaceful means, although peaceful techniques are always the first, and sometimes the best choice. Mustafa took on a certain Western cultural appearance when he immersed himself in his little shop of horrors. Cal was grateful for the room, and the mind-set. Very comforting because he knew what was coming over the horizon of the Gulf of Aden. It was the *USS Donovan,* a United States Navy warship, and the symbol of the Great Satan.

Mustafa broke the silence. "Hugh, although he has never been to my humble house, or met me before today, Cal has been an asset in this area for many years. He goes way back in the organization. He knows of all the directors, Kurt and Conrad, and his credentials are impeccable for our side. He has no politics. He has morals and ethics, but no politics. He has heard of you and your exploits, especially the situation with the woman in Barcelona a few years ago."

Hugh grimaced and turned to a laughing Mustafa, "Uncle, do we have a boat?"

"Yes, my nephew. Your cousin, Monsoor, has been able to infiltrate the local 'Al-Qaeda in Yemen' cell and has developed into quite an active, industrious lad for us. Not so much for them, but very helpful in our efforts. He may not be able to continue his association with that pack of dogs too much longer, but only time will tell. They bring dishonor upon their families in the name of Allah by distorting the Quran and its teaching for their own twisted interests. They are a cancer that must be excised."

During the last few sentences, the look of an angry, determined man crept into his eyes and features. He slowly seemed to realize Cal was intently watching his outburst. "Please forgive my passion, but these curs have cost my family dearly. Not in worldly riches, but in the lives of two of my daughters. They died when a coward left a bomb at the school my granddaughters attended."

"Uncle, do they not know Monsoor is your nephew? You are not exactly a secret to several governments and organizations."

"He has a separate identity for this. We have used this covert program a few times in the past. When this operation is complete, we will abandon the program and his undercover name will disappear."

Cal nodded in acknowledgement. The room fell quiet as the Empty Quarter in July.

Hugh broke the short silence. "Cal, my Uncle Mustafa has a varied personal history that stretches back to his younger days as a public-school student at Charterhouse, Surrey, England, followed by Oxford University and Yale, where he received his Doctorate in Chemical Engineering. While at Yale, he met several interesting individuals who were members of the 'Skull and Bones Society' who became world leaders in business and politics. Although he was not a member of their little group, he was embraced by them. Eventually, my uncle became reacquainted with some of his Oxford friends who were also friends of the Bones. One day, he was presented with an offer to assist Queen and country. He accepted and became part of an exclusive group of individuals. Uncle, how am I doing so far?"

Mustafa had been lounging in a leather chair seemingly disinterested in the historical recount of his life. He opened an eye, smiled and said, "Fairly accurate so far." He lowered his head and resumed his dispassionate façade.

"Uncle Mustafa retired from a certain British Government agency when he determined that his interests lay outside conventional political and business methods and standards. He now provides very compartmentalized contract services for our group and operates freely throughout his corner of the world."

Mustafa noisily changed position in his chair, looked at Hugh, and quietly said, "Enough stories about an old man. We need to continue our preparations. Time is passing quickly, and we have many tasks to complete."

THIRTY-NINE

The Chechen transferred from the cigarette boat to a local fishing trawler a few kilometers outside the entrance to the Port of Aden. Less than an hour later, he was safely ashore and sitting in an interior room of a house only blocks from the pier where the dhow designated to carry the explosive charges was moored. The young woman who sat across the table from him was a veteran of several campaigns against the government troops fighting for control of the country. This woman had been responsible for many enemy deaths and injuries as the result of her carefully constructed explosive weapons. The Chechen had little regard for women, in general, but this was more than just a woman, she was an experienced fighter and killer. He studied her young face for a moment, "Any problems with our plans?"

She stared directly into his eyes. They were as two sharks passing in the warm waters of a killing ground. Four lifeless eyes betraying no souls. "All is well, Why do you ask?"

"I have an uneasy feeling about this operation. Several events have recently come to pass. I cannot identify any direct relationship to our project, but something feels wrong."

The woman looked away for a moment, then returned her gaze to him, "I have no reason to believe we have issues. I have personally vetted each member of our team."

"I have issues with this, and maybe with you," he snarled. "Listen woman, you may be good with explosives, but do not contradict me. I am not in the mood."

Unflinching, she moved her fingers tighter around the grip of her Makarov pistol concealed beneath her flowing garments. She had received threats in the past from her male counterparts and was not in the mood for continued abuse. "You asked a question. I gave my answer. If you do not like the answer, do not ask the question. This is not my first time."

The Chechen returned the lifeless stare and decided not to upset the plan at this late stage. He could deal with this woman at a later time, if necessary. "We have a few hours remaining, I will carefully monitor the situation. You may go."

Rising immediately from her chair while maintaining her grip on the pistol, she took one step back, then turned and moved abruptly through the doorway and out of the room. She did not like this man and vowed to enhance his knowledge of manners when her time came.

The man stared at the empty doorway. He had sensed her disdain for him and wondered if she would really use the pistol concealed under her traditional robes. He decided she would definitely try to kill him in the future. But then he thought, *I would do the same.*

He sat for a moment then called to his two bodyguards, "Come, let us go to the mosque. I need to reflect on the day's events. They walked out of the building to a small Toyota Corolla waiting at the door to the building. "The mosque, please." They rode the rest of the way in silence.

The Chechen removed his shoes, washed his feet and donned a pair of slippers before entering the mosque as required by his religion. Carefully, scrutinizing his fellow worshippers and the surrounding space, he saw nothing that could be considered a threat. History had proven even in this holy place enemies would gladly kill. He completed his prayers then moved to a bench in a side corridor outside the main room. He sat and waited. He waited for nothing in particular other than a resolution to the nagging feeling he had about this operation. Something was unsettling, but he could not identify the cause for his apprehension. Studying a spider hanging from a silk thread near a window, he was roused by the vibration of his cell phone. Recognizing the number, he pressed the button, "Speak quickly."

The familiar voice of one of his lieutenants came clearly, "We may have a problem at the port. One of our people observed the boat owner speaking with the Aden Port Police again. Why is a known smuggler speaking with the police?"

"Because his cousin is a member of the police. He is also one of our sympathizers and a source of information. But I agree with your concern. We cannot be too careful. Have someone watch the boat and the owner until we have served Allah. You have done well." He pressed another button and ended the call, and immediately dialed another number. A cell phone in Pakistan vibrated. It was late, and the owner of the phone did not want to wake his family sleeping in the next room. Quietly, he answered, "Yes?"

The Chechen began, "I just received a call from one of my men. The boat owner has been seen meeting with the port police here. I have instructed our people to maintain a vigil on the boat and its owner until we have completed. I feel something is wrong, but I cannot be certain."

"You are well served by your caution. Continue as you have said and let me know of any anomalies." The call ended and the man returned to his bed. He endured a fitful night. He, too, was worried.

The Chechen looked at the phone in his hand and thought, *The local "Al Qaeda in Yemen" cell has claimed they are only using seasoned fighters, but this boat captain who sells the dhow is a new wrinkle. I wonder if he has any relatives other than the corrupt port police who should be examined. Maybe yes, maybe no, so I will keep this to myself until I have proof of the traitor.*

FORTY

The "Millenium" arrived on a stiff breeze charging in from the North Atlantic. Tension in the Long Island control room increased by nearly imperceptible increments when Kurt entered wearing the look of a man on a mission.

"The directors have confirmed their decision to terminate the membership of Prince Ibn Al-Wahidi and his closest associates with 'extreme prejudice.' There had been some hesitation on the part of a few members, but the unprincipled young man has now created an untenable situation within the directorate by jeopardizing the status quo. Ron, will you please begin preparations to remove Ibn Al-Wahidi from the list of active members. You will also manage the others in his close circle who have been identified as negative influences. The Directorate has summoned him and his associates to a meeting in Geneva. The prince and his party will travel on his Boeing Business Jet flown by his own crew. He does not trust anyone outside his immediate family, so one of his younger brothers will be the pilot-in-command, and a cousin will be his first officer. These two individuals are also integral parts of his organization, and act as security and assassins as well. They must be eliminated as well as the rest of his entourage. The message must be clear and decisive.

Tim, you will continue with the plan to place an explosive device on the fuel tank of the jet. Per the op order, the primary method for triggering the device will be a digital signal sent via satellite from this control room. A secondary triggering mechanism using a timing and barometric pressure sensing device has also been incorporated into the weapon. After the aircraft is airborne and on its route over the Mediterranean to Geneva, the device will be triggered. The resulting explosions will tear the wings from the fuselage, and the jet will plummet into one of the deepest undersea chasms not long after their departure. We will select the exact location after we have intercepted their approved flight plan. Unfortunately, there will be no survivors. Tim, your explosives training and experience make you our perfect choice for this task. Ron will be the Project Manager, and Eddie will provide any support you may require. Thank you."

The flat voice matched the lifeless eyes. Tim thought, *"There ARE land sharks."* Ingrid furtively examined his face and body language for an instant. He was so engrossed in the moment and Kurt's words, he failed to notice her fleeting look. The recently retired ATF Agent rapidly turned his attention to the computer screen showing the schematics of a Boeing Business Jet also known as a Boeing 737.

Ron walked over to Tim. "It was only a matter of time before this idiot Arab got to this point. He just believed his own press releases about his importance and entitlement. He was rude and treated the 'old money' with contempt. He had embarrassed family elders on more than one occasion. Ingrid had predicted his actions nearly two months ago. She certainly knows her stuff."

"Ron, is this normal for our group?"

"Yes and no. Not a daily thing, but not an isolated event." He must have recognized the look on Tim's face because he continued, "We are not in the assassination business. We are in business, and death is a tool to employ, when necessary, much the same as a corporate realignment. It is only used in an authorized operation when no other options are available. Rare, but not extraordinary. You are rapidly nearing the time when you will be authorized to develop and execute such a plan. Pardon the pun." Ron turned to walk to his desk when he focused his gaze on Tim, "One more thing. This young sociopath has singly, and fully funded at least half a dozen bombings targeting civilian locations. His most infamous include a children's hospital and a school primarily in a Shia refugee camp. He is a Sunni, but several directors are Shia Muslims. Any questions?"

Tim began to re-examine his recent move to the Directorate. He recognized the cynicism that had taken over a great part of his thought processes, but this was a step into a new, extreme world. He wondered if he could do it and began to question his choice to join this group.

The room returned to the muted background noise while each member initiated his or her operational plan checklist. Tim researched route options and identified potential locations along the proposed route for the target. They knew the departure would be from the posh island resort of Ibiza in the western Mediterranean Sea, off the eastern coast of Spain. The island is known as a place of many vices for the international entitled community. Tim reviewed the social and psychological profile of the prince and his ilk Ingrid had prepared and mused, *"Not really the place an Islamic "true believer" should visit unless he is testing the forgiveness of*

Allah and his family, but the target was not really a good example of a religious man. His lifestyle would be tested in final judgement in only a few hours, and Allah would find him lacking. He had made too many poor choices. No virgins for him or his crowd in the hereafter."

The flight was scheduled to depart from Ibiza, then follow a northern route over the western Mediterranean, before entering French airspace somewhere near Marseille on the Riviera. The best location for an accident would be about two hundred miles northeast of Ibiza, where the sea is about ten thousand feet deep. Normal flight operations would require about twenty-five minutes for takeoff, climb and cruise to that point. The Long Island control room would monitor Spanish and French air traffic control to obtain definitive flight following information. The plan identified the specific location inside the aircraft behind an inspection panel in the outer skin of the airplane where the wing meets the fuselage. That area contains the central point of the aircraft fuel tank system. A small explosion would create heat, overpressure and small pieces of debris destroying the centerline tank and the fuselage. The resulting internal explosion would move through the fuel lines to each of the other fuel tanks. No survivors. Large, dispersed wreckage field. Difficult accident investigation. Bad ending to a bad life. Maybe the Prince would meet some of his victims in the afterlife, but Tim doubted that proposition.

While Tim reviewed his portion of the plan, Eddie hacked into the Spanish air traffic control system to view the flight plan for the target. Tail number HB-IZZ, a Boeing Business Jet registered in Switzerland to an international Energy Consulting firm secretly owned by the prince, had filed its flight plan from Ibiza, Spain, to Geneva, Switzerland as a non-stop trip with an eight o'clock departure the next morning. The timetable was set. HB-IZZ would depart, climb, enter the cruise phase, and disappear from air traffic control radar while its occupants would disappear from the known world. The Directorate would call for an appropriate period of mourning. Members would whisper to each other. The "Old Guard" would send a message to be received by all directors, especially those with aspirations counter to the leadership. The Control Room would continue to operate in the same routine manner, and its workforce would continue to be paid very, very well.

Ingrid was working on satellite schedules and flight paths. She monitored several birds ensuring redundancy in the plan to send the detonation signal to the explosive device. If one bird encountered a problem and could not be used to transmit the signal, she needed to identify at least two back-ups and pass the information to Eddie. That system was backstopped with the old-school barometric pressure sensing device and a clock.

Additionally, she followed explicit directions from Kurt and Conrad. *"Monitor Tim and provide a psychological post-mortem after completion of the current operation."*

FORTY-ONE

All was going as planned in Aden. Mustafa was working with some chemicals in the lab. A careful man, he donned the appropriate gloves, supplied air breathing equipment, apron and splash shield. He introduced a stabilizing component into the chemical compound to create a material that could be safely transported. If the compound worked as planned, the bonding material between the boards of the hull would liquefy and dissolve, thereby allowing water to seep into the boat. The boat would become too heavy and sink before it reached the US warship.

Hugh and Cal were reviewing the plan for Hugh to get onto the boat before Al-Qaeda could place the explosives on board. Cal would provide cover from a building overlooking the pier where the boat was moored for loading. Inspecting the gun cabinet, Cal had chosen an Accuracy International, Model L115A3 rifle, the standard issue sniper rifle of the British Military, with a bipod, silencer, and Schmidt & Bender scope. He had used the weapon on many occasions as a consultant for several government agencies. Cal hefted the weapon and smiled, "Mustafa, you are a true connoisseur of military weaponry. I congratulate you."

Mustafa modestly replied, "We try. We try." Rising from his stool at the fume hood, he looked at Hugh and Cal, and softly proclaimed, "I must pray now", and he quietly left the room.

Cal looked at a map and satellite photos of the pier selected as the launch site for the attack on *The Sullivans*. "Do you have a perch for my position?"

Hugh walked to the table, bent over the photos, and pointed to a building at the top of a sharply rising escarpment across the road from the dock. "This building has an access from the back side of the hill. You can use that entry during the early morning hours while the sky is still dark. Monsoor will deliver you to the building and provide the key for the door. After you are safely delivered, he will go to the boat to begin his watch. He is night security for ALQaeda in Yemen."

Cal studied the images. The building provided an excellent location.

Hugh straightened up and stretched. "I will wear Arab clothing, ride a motorbike to the location, meet Monsoor, go onto the boat and apply the chemicals in the appropriate locations. The boat is about eighteen meters long, so my job will be complete within about fifteen minutes after boarding. You will be my final security. The explosives are scheduled to arrive at the boat about an hour after I complete my work. Monsoor will have a communications chip implanted under his skin behind his ear so you will be able to hear any conversations and provide any information you discover at the scene. He will be relieved of his duty before sunrise prayers."

FORTY-TWO

Ingrid walked into the control room pushing a small cart filled with water, coffee, juices, sandwiches, pastries, and an old-fashioned glass bottle of milk in an ice bucket. "If we are to be here for a while, this should help keep our caloric intake high enough to function. Conrad happened to be in the kitchen when I was collecting this gourmet feast. He looks more worried than I have ever seen. Aside from the usual operational jitters, he is uneasy about Al Qaeda assets at Emirates Airlines. Especially at JFK."

Eddie chimed in from his console, "Why do you think he's worried? Is he wearing different colored socks?"

Ingrid looked at Eddie with the expression of a dismayed mother. "You are perfectly correct. He is wearing one black and one blue."

Properly chastised, Eddie sheepishly returned to his work at the computer.

Kurt walked into the room just as Ingrid had finished her retort. "Yes, Conrad is worried, but he is also color blind. Occasionally, that dress code violation occurs. Does that satisfy your curiosity, Eddie? The directors have expressed their concern over the potential loss of life resulting from the pending aircraft affair. We need to confirm the crew and passenger manifest, to ensure only targeted personnel are on board. Eddie, please contact the usual asset to accomplish that task. Tim, any change in departure or route data?"

"No changes. The French are usually very anal about flight plan changes into their homeland from any source other than another Frenchman. They especially enjoy screwing with the Swiss and the Americans. Possibly, the French still hold a grudge concerning Swiss sympathy toward the Germans in 'WW Two', and how they managed cash, gold and art stolen from the French. I'm still not sure about their attitude toward the good old USA."

Kurt feigned a pained expression. "We have many prominent French directors. I would hope you are not insulting their character or lineage."

Ron burst into a massive grin. "Kurt, really sorry about that display of emotion, but when a German defends the French, I find it incredibly hilarious. Please forgive me."

Kurt smiled. This time it was a warm smile. "I am offended to the core that you should believe the Germans hold that particular view, but enough sarcasm, we need to complete the tasks before us, including the question of the manifest."

Ingrid was back at her console. "Our source has confirmed the occupants of the Boeing. Only the target and his family members are listed. No innocents."

Kurt replied, "Thank you, Ingrid. Now I must pass this information to Conrad and the directorate.

Ron asked Ingrid and Eddie to confirm their preparations for the satellite communications up-link from Aden. Both reported communications to the primary satellite, and the two back-ups were operating without any problems.

Ron, as the primary position for the Aden operation, would make all decisions as the mission director.

Kurt looked at everyone in the room. "Eat now, and relax until we start the last phase of the Aden op." He left to meet with Conrad.

FORTY-THREE

Aden was nearly ready to begin its metamorphosis from inky black night to gray twilight. Only a little more than two hours of complete darkness before the city would begin its normal transition to a bustling, dusty, dirty ancient port city. Hugh and Cal were awake and ready even though the hands of the clock on the wall were quietly creeping up on four in the morning, Hugh busily created his Arab persona while Cal carefully prepared his equipment. Mustafa silently padded into the room in his traditional robe and a pair of well-worn, elegant red leather slippers. Cal looked at the slippers. Mustafa looked down, smiled, and said, "My 'Good Luck' slippers. Always wear them for the operational phase of an assignment. They were a gift from an old friend many years ago when I was much younger. Everyone and everything have stories. Theses slippers and I have fond memories." He turned and left the room.

When he returned, Monsoor was with him. The young man looked at the two operatives with eyes that belied intelligence, competence, and intensity. He looked "right." Not in a suicidal way, but in a professional manner. He was ready. He nodded to Mustafa who asked Cal, "Are you ready?"

The old warrior looked at his equipment, "Yes. I have everything I need."

Cal and Monsoor left the room. Mustafa watched Hugh become another person. A chameleon. Hugh looked at him with a lifeless, grisly façade. "I'll be ready in just a minute."

Mustafa walked over to a locked safe, opened the door, removed a stainless-steel container that looked much like a thermos bottle, and placed it on the table in front of Hugh. "This will work. I have successfully used this compound on several past occasions, and it has never failed." After examining the container, he pronounced, "All is ready. You have been instructed on its use. I can do nothing further but wish you luck and pray for you."

Hugh placed the container in his backpack and walked to the door. "I will wait for Monsoor in the courtyard."

The moonless, night sky was full of stars that provided no light. Perfect night to move through the city. Fishermen would be rising soon but would not yet move to their boats. Mugs of tea, breakfast and prayers all came first.

Monsoor solemnly drove the small brown truck through the empty streets of Aden. It was an unobtrusive truck, a good truck, a truck with a hidden compartment. Cal calmly rested in the passenger seat, looked at the passing buildings, scrub trees, debris and dirt as the truck easily climbed the hill. The narrow lane turned sharply to the right and ended at the door of a drab, commercial building in an obvious state of disrepair. With Hugh still safely ensconced in the rear of the truck, Monsoor shut off the engine, walked to the steel door, unlocked a padlock and waved at Cal to join him. The young Arab nodded at a set of stairs. "We will go to the top floor where you will find an unlocked window. In the hallway outside the door will be bags of sand for construction. You can use them as your shooting base. After you have seen the room and confirmed all is ready, I will depart to join my Al Qaeda 'friends' at the dock. Five minutes after Hugh has completed his tasks on the boat, and all is clear, you will return to the door where an oil company truck will be waiting for you. Mustafa has arranged for a driver to return you to his home. The driver is the son of his oldest cousin." Monsoor padded down the stairs, left the building and climbed into the truck for his short journey to the place from which he had "borrowed" the truck.

Cal set up his perch. Hopefully, he would not need the rifle. If he needed to abort, he would go to a tunnel under the main stairs that led to the next building to wait until contacted via the earpiece lodged in his right ear.

FORTY-FOUR

An hour before sunrise, the Chechen sat up on his cot. He suffered a bad night, sleeping in fits and starts. The man could not resolve his inner misgivings about the imminent operation. The boat had been purchased, and the local Al Qaeda in Yemen cell was providing constant security at the dock. He had vetted the former owner of the dhow and his ties to the Aden Port Police and decided the boat owner and his cousins as well as the rest of the Port Police were as corrupt as any in that part of the world. He had personally examined the explosives to be loaded onto the dhow and had reviewed the detonation systems with the insolent woman. Hesitating for only an instant, he grabbed his cell phone and called his man positioned at dockside watching the dhow and its security. He punched a series of numbers into the phone and waited for an answer. Less than one ring later, a gruff male voice responded, "Yes?"

"Anything out of the norm?"

"No. The local man has been attentive. He has not fallen asleep and has challenged two men who walked along the pier to another craft a short distance away. No police or Yemen Customs patrol craft in the area. The Infidels are moored at the proper location, fully exposed to our plan. All seems to be quiet on the ship. The new security person has arrived for the change. Everything appears to be in good order. We will speak again very soon."

"Good. continue your watch. We have only a few hours remaining." The phone call quickly ended without the customary Arabic "good-byes" or other comment.

The Chechen sat on the edge of his cot and stared at the wall, then stood and dressed in his traditional garb. He would go to the mosque one last time before the operation, then go to the dock and watch the operation from a safe distance. He told himself, *I am not a coward, but the movement cannot lose my talents. I must survive unless we find no other alternative.* Ten minutes later, he and his bodyguards walked out into the dark, cold, damp morning to walk to the mosque at the end of the lane. He would break his fast after the target was destroyed.

FORTY-FIVE

The biting, damp, frigid winds and cruel salt spray slashing at the Long Island manor house was typical for the season, but Tim never felt any of it while sitting at his console monitoring Spanish Flight Service. It was late. He was tired, but excited. Considerable activity was happening that actually made a difference to so many, both good and bad. No changes with the air traffic controllers, or the system. Usually, no changes would come, if at all, until about an hour before departure. But he watched anyway.

Eddie and Ingrid worked at their stations. Eddie continued his hack into the necessary satellite programs while Ingrid worked the communications protocols to establish contact with the op in Aden. Ingrid, her headset in place, hit the transmit button to establish encoded communication with Aden. Mustafa replied with two clicks. Hugh and Cal responded in the same manner when prompted. Ingrid spoke into her microphone to the others monitoring the intercom function within the control room. Eddie, Ron, and Tim checked in. They could talk privately to each other using the intercom function.

Ron began the operational control room procedures with the formal check-in. Each position responded.

Eddie started with, "I have the primary bird on-line, with two others on standby. If the first fails, we can immediately switch to the next. We should not have a problem. The NRO does good work." The *National Reconnaissance Office*, NRO, the agency responsible for the United States surveillance satellite program had no clue their equipment had been hacked and hijacked for a few minutes. Since the NRO is not officially associated with the Directorate, or its control room, these actions would be considered a national security violation, and a crime. Eddie was thrilled to be doing something illegal, and the fact that he was being paid for it was just a bonus.

Ingrid came on-line next. "I have established voice and data connections. No problems."

Tim came on last. "No changes."

Ron opened another internal channel. "Conrad, Kurt, Control is ready. Communications established, and all portions of op plan proceeding on schedule. We're green."

Two clicks from Kurt, and three clicks from Conrad, confirmed their receipt of the message.

Tim was a bit confused. Why is Ingrid performing technical and operational duties when she is a Behavioral Scientist? *"I need to ask Ron about this interesting situation."*

The young Monsoor took a little detour on his Vespa scooter from his direct route to his next stop, the house of his uncle and a meeting with a man named Hugh. He was nervous. This was a bigger assignment than he had ever been given. The early hours of the morning were cool, but a sheen of cold sweat covered his entire body. After the second turn, a pair of headlights shone at a steady distance behind him. Only one set of lights, but the hour was too early for many trucks or cars to be on the road. In an hour, things would be different. He turned into a lane leading to another larger road. He could watch where the lane met the new road. He parked behind a wall and stood on top of a pile of bricks watching the small intersection. Seconds later, a compact sedan came into view and slowed to a crawl. The sole occupant sat in the car, looked both ways then drove away from Monsoor. He waited. Maybe the car would return. A few minutes later, he decided to resume his circuitous route. He checked his watch. Time was quickly passing.

As he moved through the streets, nothing else out of the ordinary happened. He was still scared, but the sweating stopped, and his heart rate slowed as he approached his destination. When he turned into the lane leading to Mustafa and safety, he saw a lone figure standing in the shadows of the wall. His heart stopped, and he nearly lost control of the Vespa. Then he recognized Hugh in his Arab clothing and continued to the gate. Hugh motioned him through the entrance.

"The Peace be upon you, Monsoor."

"Wa-Alaikum-Salaam."

Hugh looked at the young man. "Are you okay? You look a bit stressed."

The young man motioned to Hugh, "Come. Let us go inside. I must speak with you and Mustafa. I had a strange occurrence on my way back here."

They found Mustafa in the garden resting in a rattan chair near the fountain. He took them into the safe room where Monsoor recounted his experience. Hugh and Mustafa looked at each other. Mustafa spoke first. "We have no credible information indicating the plan has been compromised. None of our assets report any problems. Hugh what do you think?"

Hugh leaned against a table near the door. "I think we have no reason to abort. We have reason to be more watchful, and we should advise Control and ask if they have any reason to abort."

Mustafa surveyed the ceiling for a moment. "If Control had any issues, we would be contacted. We will press forward with the schedule, but I will advise them of this new information, and our decision to continue with no changes." He turned to Monsoor. "Are you ready?"

He spoke quietly, "Yes. Yes, I am."

They walked out of the house to the courtyard where Monsoor had parked a small van he used as his regular transportation. Hugh climbed into the rear of the van and opened the door to the secret compartment where he would ride as they moved toward the target through the deserted streets.

Monsoor eased the truck through the gate and into the lane. The chemical compound Hugh carried in the container would destroy the hull, and the ever-lethal Hugh would destroy anything, or anyone, that might jeopardize the mission.

FORTY-SIX

Khallad stood quietly in his room in the early morning and felt uneasy. The potential leak was not an uncommon issue in any plan as intricate as this. Operational security was always a concern, and he had experienced these same misgivings many times in the past. With a heavy sigh, he phoned his local Al Qaeda in Yemen contact. Two rings later the contact answered the phone. "Yes."

Without the typical greetings Khallad spoke, "Is everything set?"

"Yes, we have the product ready for delivery to the shipper. Our installation men are ready for the next phase."

He hesitated to ask the next question, but believed it necessary, "We believe one of our competitors has made an attempt to disrupt our supply chain. Do you have any indications this is true?"

The voice responded flatly, "No, all is well. I share your concern, but we have no information regarding that potential issue. I repeat, no information."

"Very well but maintain vigilance." He ended the call, but still remained uneasy. He quickly made another call. Once again, no traditional greeting, "I need you to come to my location. We may have a security breach. The local manager insists we have no supply chain concerns, but I want you to meet me in half an hour. Be prepared for any problems."

The man at the other end responded, "I will see you shortly."

Less than a mile away from the docks, a solitary figure in traditional clothing eased into a small, non-descript sedan and drove quickly through the darkened, sleeping streets of the city to an empty building near the dhow. The man had been sent on the mission by his brother, the Chechen, to watch the dhow and the approach to the dock.

Mustafa called Long Island on the secure telephone, relayed the information concerning Monsoor, and that the op had been set into motion. Cal was ready at his position. Monsoor and Hugh were driving toward the target. Mustafa had his local assets ready if needed. When Ron received the call, he opened the channel so the rest of the team could monitor the conversation. He acknowledged the information, and immediately contacted Kurt.

Kurt and Conrad came into the control room. Both men looked grim. Kurt had decided not to interfere in the Aden situation. He and Conrad were present to monitor circumstances, not to micro-manage.

Kurt spoke, "Have you noted any anomalies, inconsistencies or unusual communication traffic?"

Every member of the Control Room staff reported no issues. Ron, the team leader, stood, "Kurt, we have had some com traffic, but nothing out of the ordinary, and nothing from our voice recognition software. At this point, I believe we have not been compromised."

Conrad quietly stepped forward, "Mustafa called to confirm the initiation of the final phase of the operation. Please go back to work. Thank you."

FORTY-SEVEN

Monsoor drove the specially modified truck directly to the pier to relieve one of the local Al-Qaeda cell members who had been on duty all night. The guard greeted Monsoor, told him the night had been quiet and drove away on his motorcycle.

Hugh monitored the changing of the guard via his earpiece while Cal listened to the conversations from his vantage point using the satellite communications equipment provided by control and watched the men through his rifle-mounted scope.

When the motorcycle was safely clear, Monsoor slid into the truck. Two minutes later, Hugh edged out of the secret compartment and eased from the truck through the driver's door. Anyone watching would have thought Monsoor was leaving the truck. Hugh walked swiftly to the boat, went below into the hold and went to work on the hull. Twelve minutes later, he returned to the truck, and eased into the compartment. Monsoor got out of the truck, carefully studied the area then walked to the boat.

Less than a minute after the young man reached the dhow, Cal sensed movement to the left of the boat. He moved his sighting scope to the area of interest but could not find anything amiss. He then pulled out a small nightscope from inside his jacket, steadied the device on a sandbag and watched the darkened area. Then he saw it. A slight shift in the shadows. The sniper began to reach for the rifle when the shadow became more defined. Seconds later, he saw the large alley cat creep into full view. The denizen of the night scanned the area, much as Cal had done a few seconds earlier, then moved off away from the truck and the scene returned to normal. One more scan of the area and he could relax a bit. He searched the same spot when he saw it, more movement in the shadows a short distance from the truck. He could not really identify the anomaly, but something was wrong. Less than a heartbeat later, he spotted another change in the shadows and the glow from the tip of a cigarette. No cat this time. Someone was hidden amongst a group of boxes near the pier. He lifted the rifle to his shoulder and peered through the scope. At first, he could not locate the potential intruder, but after a few seconds, the individual moved out of the shadows and into the open under a lamp post. The target stood motionless looking toward Monsoor and the boat. Cal rested the barrel of the rifle on the sandbags to steady his sight picture. Cal spoke quietly into his transmitter. "We have an unknown subject on the pier watching the boat. I don't know how long he has been there, but I just discovered his presence. No overt act, yet."

On the other side of the world Ron sat upright in his chair and Mustafa became more alert at his home. Cal continued his watch, and Hugh tensed. Monsoor continued to sit quietly on the stern rail of the boat, not giving any indication that someone was watching him. Cal thought, *Monsoor, you are a very cool customer. Don't lose it now.*

The intruder looked over his shoulder and began walking to the boat. The radio chatter had alerted Monsoor, so he was ready when the intruder appeared in the dim light of an overhead street lamp and said, "As-salamu alaykum, Monsoor."

Monsoor responded, "Wa-Alaikum-Salaam."

"It is me, Ahmed Hamzi."

Here was one of the upper echelon field agents in Al-Qaeda in Yemen. He was also one of its most violent members. He enjoyed killing and maiming with a knife and had more than a few notches on his knife handle.

Monsoor maintained his composure. "Ahmed, good to see you. I had no idea someone would be here to help me. Thank you."

Hugh, still hidden in the truck, considered his options. If the situation did not escalate, he would do nothing. If things "went sideways", either Cal or he would act. That would generate another set of issues. He waited for Ahmed to make the next move.

Ahmed peered intently at the guard, "Why did you enter the boat? You were inside for over ten minutes."

Monsoor gave his reply without hesitation, "I was curious. I wanted to see what was in there."

Ahmed pressed, "It took you ten minutes to look inside such a small craft?"

This was not going well. The answers did not seem to satisfy Ahmed. He looked directly at Monsoor, and angrily growled, "I do not believe you. Something is wrong here."

Cal heard them exchanging unintelligible foreign words. He tightened his grip on the rifle stock and slid his finger onto the trigger. He knew that Ahmed would be dead in an instant if the confrontation escalated too much more.

At the same time, Hugh was silently moving out of the truck through the rear door which he had left slightly ajar just for this possibility. Now clad in a black shirt, shoes and pants, he moved silently on soft rubber soled shoes to a position just behind the threat. Ahmed became more inflamed as he berated Monsoor. The young man held his position at the stern rail as Ahmed's emotions caused him to fully center his wrath and concentration on Monsoor. He was so distracted that he did not hear or see Hugh stealthily moving through the darkness behind several large, wooden crates.

Ahmed had been menacingly pointing a finger on his left hand at Monsoor, but now his right hand was moving toward his body, and the large knife on his belt.

Cal and Hugh simultaneously saw the first movements toward the knife. Cal was about to squeeze the trigger on his silenced sniper rifle when he saw Hugh fly into view. Hugh effortlessly lunged forward, using his left hand to push his victim's head forward with an upward knife thrust into the back of the neck where the number one vertebra meets the base of the skull. The severed spinal cord resulted in a clean, quiet kill. The late Ahmed Hamzi dropped instantly and lifelessly to the ground. No loud cries for help, no blood, just a limp body to manage.

Hugh spoke quietly. "Control, we have a package to manage. The op has not been compromised. We will remove the item and contact you with further information." His mind raced as he looked for a place to permanently dispose of the late Ahmed. When they first arrived at the pier, he had checked the area for people and things. The professional term is "Situational Awareness." The night sky was still jet black, but dawn would come before too long. He checked his watch and noted he had about forty-five minutes before the night started to lift and the area would teem with fishermen and dock workers. He looked to the east and spotted the rusting coastal trawler that would complete his plan for Ahmed.

Hugh turned to Monsoor, "Do you see any rope on this boat?"

"Yes, there are several coils in the hold."

"If you would please bring up a ten-foot piece of rope, I will use it to dispose of our friend."

Hugh removed the clothing from the body of the late Ahmed and found his cell phone. The power was on, so GPS tracking was possible. He left the power on and placed the phone on the dock next to the dhow. Monsoor brought the rope to Hugh who then tied the rope around the neck of the naked body, eased the corpse into the murky harbor, and began to swim to the trawler with his package in tow. Darkness continued to cover the harbor and all its environs. Hugh silently swam to the stern of the shabby coastal trawler, treaded water and waited for any sounds to come from the ship. The deadly stillness filled the air except for the occasional clank of a chain banging on a rail. Hugh took a deep breath and dove the few feet below the murky surface to wrap the rope around the propeller housing and shaft. He came to the surface and listened again for a few moments. When satisfied all was well, he pulled the rope taut around the shaft and watched the body sliding below the surface to only twelve inches from the propeller blades. One last dive to secure the rope, and he swam away from the body and moved smoothly back to the dhow. Ten minutes later, he broke the surface at the edge of the dock.

Cal watched the entire scene through his rifle scope as he kept his finger near the trigger guard, ready to act if necessary. So far, he had not seen anything that would jeopardize the operation. He continued to watch and wait.

Hugh smoothly slipped out of the water, picked up the cell phone and clothing, and climbed into the cargo area of the truck. He looked at the items recently owned by Ahmed and considered the next part of his plan. He thought, *After Monsoor is replaced by the next Al-Qaeda operative, we will drive to the Russian Embassy located only a few kilometers from the pier. We will place the cell phone near the entrance to the compound. If Al-Qaeda wanted to locate Ahmed, his cell phone would place him at the Russian Embassy."* Hugh mused, "A little diversion never hurt anyone."

Hugh transmitted his plan to all members so they would know what was about to happen. The only change to the plan entailed Eddie remotely downloading and copying the data from the cell phone for intelligence purposes and leaving the phone number and other identifying information intact so that if the number were called, the phone remained linked to Ahmed.

The former Al Qaeda operative was about to become chum for the denizens of Aden Harbor courtesy of the propeller blades of a certain coastal trawler.

Thirty minutes later, three trucks pulled up to the pier next to the boat, and Monsoor exchanged greetings with an unknown individual. The young man was directed to leave before the explosives were loaded onto the boat. He gratefully complied and drove away with Hugh safely hidden in the secret compartment.

When Monsoor and Hugh safely drove away from the dock, Cal disassembled the rifle, and placed it into his backpack. He replaced the sandbags to their original location in the hall, walked down the stairs and waited for the truck. A few minutes later, the oil company truck appeared. He climbed into the passenger seat for an uneventful ride back to Mustafa.

By the time the saboteurs began loading the explosives onto the boat, the chemical compound had begun its work. The wooden boards of the hull were beginning to fail. The leaks began as a small, unnoticeable, damp spots. Thirty minutes later, and only several meters from the dock, the heavily laden dhow mysteriously settled below the gently lapping waves. The *USS Donovan* left port without a scratch.

The late morning sun flashed overhead when the engines of a derelict coastal trawler docked a short distance from the sunken dhow turned its first revolutions of the day only to find its propeller fouled by a piece of rope tangled in the blades and wrapped around the shaft. The crewman tapped to fix the problem panicked when he discovered a section of rope and a human leg jammed in the metal structure supporting the propeller shaft. After removing the rope and leg, the smugglers operating the trawler decided not to involve the police who might ask questions and inspect the ship, so they slowly steamed out of the harbor. Just before evening prayers that day the trawler anchored just off a sparsely populated section of the Somali coast to deliver its load of contraband to a band of pirates.

FORTY-EIGHT

The Chechen furiously slammed his fist on the bare wooden table in a house at an Aden fishing dock near where the dhow had recently sunk. "What happened! You are the supposed leader of this cell and operation. You and your people have failed," he screamed at the young woman.

She returned his fiery gaze with a slow, steady stream of Arabic words and phrases not usually heard from such a petite woman. "We provided security, but your man was to have overseen the loading operation. Where is he? You are the mastermind, and he was your man. But he was not here. He is missing. Is this how you run your operation? Do not chastise me, you arrogant fool. Your people failed this operation."

The Chechen and his two men were outnumbered and outgunned in the small room. He felt the anger boiling in his throat, but controlled his temper, "You will retrieve the explosives for another time. We are not done here." Those last word were not lost on the woman. She knew he directed the statement toward the operation and her, too.

The three Al Qaeda men left the building and drove back to a new temporary location to lick their wounds and report to Khallad. It would not be a pleasant phone call.

FORTY-NINE

Conrad and Kurt walked throughout the control room congratulating each of the staff. Conrad was beaming, "Lady and Gentlemen, the Directors are extremely satisfied with your results in Yemen. You will see a substantial deposit into each of your bank accounts, but we cannot rest on our laurels. The second phase of the operation regarding Ibiza remains on your schedule. I believe Tim shall be leaving for the airport and our business jet in a short while. Team, please continue the good work. Thank you for your efforts."

Conrad quickly vanished from the room leaving Kurt standing in front of the large computer screen on the wall. "Ron, Tim, will you join me in the library in an hour? We need to discuss some items."

Ron and Tim sat at their consoles in their chairs. Ron turned toward Tim, "Hey partner, let's get something from the kitchen. OK?"

Tim eased out his chair and caught a glimpse of Ingrid watching him.

The men sat on wooden bar stools at the large kitchen worktable in the center of the room. "Tim, what do you think of this place so far? Have you had a chance to form any opinions or thoughts?"

Tim studied the shiny, stainless-steel countertop for a few seconds, "I haven't had time to decide anything other than this job pays well, and several of my colleagues are 'eccentric' at best."

Ron nodded, "I guess you're right on both parts. But I was thinking more about some of the measures used to gain our required results."

"If you mean intentionally killing people, then I really haven't had the time for an in-depth consideration. The house and grounds are certainly over-the-top for a lowly civil servant, and the people are still open to review, but I'm working on it."

Ron sighed deeply, "I completely understand. I really do. My first few days on the job were much quieter and simpler. At first, I wondered if this was more than a mundane 'desk job', but eventually I came to the same crossroad you are nearing. My decision was a personal choice, and you will need to do the same, only on a more accelerated schedule.' He hesitated, "I am violating a confidence, but we go back too many years, so here it is. Have you figured out what function Ingrid performs for our little group? Although she has several roles, one of her most important to the Directorate is the mental health and stability of our people. She is our psychological internal affairs. Do you remember the Strategic Air Command, nuclear weapons Human Reliability Program where everyone watched for mental instability in everyone else? Well, Ingrid is our local version. I imagine Kurt has tasked her with determining whether you can be a successful member of the team in all facets of every operation. I stress, 'All Facets' of what we do here. Do you understand?"

Frowning, Tim quietly said, "I know what you mean. I wondered why she was looking at me like a lab specimen after Kurt went into more detail on my part in the next phase of this operation. I didn't think she was checking me out as a potential partner."

Both men sat quietly at the counter when approaching footsteps clicked on the polished concrete floor.

"Hello, gentlemen, am I interrupting?" came the pleasant female voice from the kitchen entrance. Ingrid walked past the two men sitting at the counter and went directly to a large commercial refrigerator. Without turning, she asked the men, "Can I get you anything?"

Tim walked to the large stainless coffee urn and looked back at the gentle voice, "Nothing for me, thanks."

Ron squirmed on his chair, "Same for me. Ingrid, how is your day going? Anything exciting or special?"

Still engrossed in her romp through the refrigerator, "Nothing you would be interested in hearing. Just trying to get through the day, but thanks for asking." Holding a small bottle of cranberry juice in her right hand, she closed the large stainless-steel door, turned toward the two men, and smiled. "Tim, Any thoughts on your new job here at the directorate? I think you may be having one of the more rapid introductions. Many things happening in a very short time. Whenever you have some time, we should get to know each other a little better. The stress of the control room hardly leaves time for a normal conversation. Bye guys."

The psychological interloper waved and seemed to float through the door leaving the two men looking at each other.

Ron grinned, "Tim, I believe Ingrid has begun her psychological analysis." With only a slight hesitation, he continued, "Or maybe she really meant what she said."

"Terrific, but I still don't understand why she works at a computer console in the control room when she is a behavioral clinician."

Ron shifted on his bar stool. "Ingrid discovered a talent for the complexities of operational control. She likes to juggle the many facets of a real-time situation. Initially, she was compartmentalized into 'psy-ops' and counter- intelligence functions, but Kurt and Conrad soon recognized her other talents. Of course, she still does all the psych evaluations of targets, assets and employees, but she is also very good at command center functions. I don't think anyone has really gotten close to her or understands her motivations. But she does her job and does it very well. Don't forget, she is continually evaluating each of us as she goes through her daily command center interactions and observations. Does that clear up your concerns?"

Tim smiled weakly, "No, not really. It seems a little unnerving to be the subject of a continual behavioral examination."

Ron's demeanor turned more serious, "Don't forget, her job is to get inside the heads of our friends and enemies to identify their strengths and weaknesses. It's her job to know them better than they know themselves and I've noticed she is quite excellent at that."

After a quick snack in the kitchen, Tim sat at his control room desk and waited for Ron to return from taking care of some personal business with one of his offshore bank accounts. Ron had more than one account in more than one bank, a system Tim would soon initiate for himself. The control room had become a more familiar place for the newly minted member of the Directorate. The "rookie" was more relaxed, but sensed he was experiencing a growing undercurrent of anxiety rattling around in his brain. Whenever he thought about his imminent task in the next phase of the operation, a scintilla of doubt crept into the hidden corners of his consciousness. He thought, *Maybe, this is not such a good place for me. I have been the primary and secondary cause for death throughout my working life, but this seems different. Maybe because I am about to do something for money and not an idea, although I did get paid by the Government for what I did.* Gradually, an uneasy feeling washed over him.

"Tim, where is Ron?" a familiar gentle voice asked from somewhere behind him. He turned and saw Ingrid standing a few feet from his desk.

Tim spun his chair to face the voice, "I'm not certain, but I believe he is in his private rooms doing some personal business. He should be down here in a few minutes."

She smiled warmly, hesitated, turned, and walked out of the room.

In spite of his internal control mechanism, Tim found himself watching the woman as she retreated from the room. For a moment, his mind wandered, *Is she evaluating me like an insect under a microscope, or does she really want to get to know me better. Have I been alone for too long?* For a fleeting instant he hoped it was the latter. Time to prepare for his trip and first field operation in his new job.

FIFTY

Tim, in the co-pilot seat, looked at the clock on the instrument panel of the silver and white Gulfstream V business jet as it touched down at the Ibiza airport and taxied to the darkened southwest Executive Jet ramp. Spanish Customs and Immigration believed the crew carried specialized parts for a computerized manufacturing process. In reality, the special computer parts were part of an explosive device to be placed inside the belly of a private passenger jet. The last hint of daylight barely washed over a black Boeing Business Jet, the private version of the 737, parked at the edge of the tarmac next to a bright red Cessna Citation. Security lights on the poles at the edges of the ramp provided less than adequate lighting, but he could still make out the aircraft through the night mist. In accordance with instructions from the Ibiza Ground Controller, the captain taxied the Directorate jet to a parking spot next to the Boeing jet. Apparently, the Directorate had influence down to airplane parking locations. The pilot looked over at Tim, "I delivered you, now the rest is up to you. I'm not exactly sure what you do, and I really don't care to know. We leave in four hours. Here comes Spanish Customs and Immigration."

Tim eased out of his seat and walked to the rear passenger compartment while the two pilots went out to meet the Spanish officials. As soon as the crew walked across the parking ramp with the Spanish officials, Tim began his next phase. He knew the Directorate had arranged for Spanish Customs and Immigration to ignore an interior inspection of the jet, so he pulled on dark gray coveralls and began to inventory his tools and package. The hour was late, but the airport fuel truck lumbered out to fill the thirsty jet. Twenty minutes later, the yellow tanker truck returned to the maintenance area and the driver went into his office. Tim went over the plan in his head as he had done many times during the flight over the Atlantic. The clandestine operative, for that was his new title, decided to get some sleep while he waited for quietest time of the night.

Khallad hesitated to make the call. He knew the prince would not be happy with the failure to sink the *USS Donovan,* but he must make the call. He studied the burner phone in his hand, then punched in the phone number. Five rings later the voice he recognized said, "Yes?"

The Al Qaeda operative did not fear this man, but he was an important funding source that must not be angered or discouraged. Cash flow was necessary to the success of the *jihad.* "Your highness, I have some news from our project near the gulf. Will you please turn on the encoder." Khallad could hear faint Arabic curses, then the multi-tones indicating the phones were in the secure, scrambled mode.

"Khallad, can you hear me?"

"Yes, your highness. I shall come to the point. Our mission was not successful. The dhow loaded with explosives sunk just after leaving the dock. The load was too heavy for the craft. We will be able to recover the entire load for later use against the *USS Cole* when it visits the same location in several weeks."

"What do you mean it sank!" the prince screamed into the phone. "I paid for success, not failure. This is your fault. I should have run this operation myself."

He seemed to have momentarily exhausted his rage when Khallad quickly spoke, "This is not a failure, it is only a delay. Everything went according to plan except that our people were too enthusiastic and loaded too much. They intended to inflict excessive damage to the ship and its crew. I cannot fault them for that."

The prince was not happy, but he lowered his voice, "I understand their zeal, but I cannot countenance failure. When will I see a tangible result of my investment?"

"Our sources state the USS Cole will visit the same dock in about a month. The specific date has not yet been determined, but the visit will happen. The US Government has no idea we were only minutes from success. They remain unaware of our actions. I have every confidence our quest will succeed very soon."

The prince shot back, "You had better be right." The connection ended with a decisive, metallic click.

The prince dialed a new number into the same phone. Three rings later, his uncle, Prince bin Alkanor, calmly answered, "Yes, what do you want. I told you not to ever use this number."

"Uncle, this is an emergency. Our operation in the southern gulf has failed."

The older man was incensed, "I don't know who this is. Do not ever call me again." His ear was again subjected to a loud metallic click.

Alkanor shook his head, tried to calm his anger at the young prince, and stared out his apartment windows at the blue water of the Persian Gulf. Standing in the warm sunlight he thought, *If I am not careful, This young fool is going to get me killed. I only hope it will be swift. I will not accept any more calls from this arrogant imbecile.*

Eddie sat in front of his computer on Long Island monitoring the Ibiza operation when a chime tone interrupted his concentration. The upper right corner of his computer monitor flashed a warning icon indicating an important piece of data had been intercepted from a phone call. He entered a series of keystrokes and text information from the intercept came onto the screen. He read the text to himself, then called out to Ingrid and Ron sitting at their stations and called Kurt and Conrad on the intercom. Our wayward prince has just completed two phone calls. One from Khallad and the second to his uncle Alkanor discussing the failure at the Port of Aden. I printed a hard copy of the information. The directors will not be happy about this."

Kurt and Conrad came into the control room from different directions. Conrad looked at Kurt, "I believe this has cemented our justification for the Ibiza operation and the fate of the young prince and his uncle. The Prime director will need to determine whether the information is passed to any government, but I am certain the other members of the

Directorate will be given enough detail to serve as a 'teaching moment'."

Kurt nodded, said nothing and strode out of the room. Conrad thanked the team, stared at the information still displayed on the computer screen, then walked out.

FIFTY-ONE

The alarm stirred Tim from his sleep, he checked his watch. The green and black dial glowed eerily in the darkness. He had slept until a few minutes past 3 AM. He peered out into the night and was met with murky, billowy gray cloud hugging the glistening concrete parking ramp. He softly moved to the other side of the fuselage and was greeted with the same situation. Fog. He had not considered fog as a factor but welcomed the opaque mist that would conceal his short journey to the Boeing parked next to him. But then the old pilot adage popped into his head, *If they can't see me, I can't see them.* Since noise seems to travel faster and more clearly in the fog, he still had to be careful. Hand tools, night vision goggles, the special box and the blasting cap tucked safely in his pockets, the middle-aged man moved to the aircraft door.

Inside the Executive Terminal the two security guards for the prince tried to watch the Boeing Business Jet with binoculars and night vision equipment. Spanish Officials had confined their movements to the small terminal thwarting Amir and Karim from going to the parking ramp to stand guard at the jet as demanded by the prince. The dense fog creating zero visibility prompted the duo to develop a plan to foil the Spaniards. They decided one of them should sneak onto the ramp to obey orders and avoid his wrath. Besides, what could the Spanish do to them, send them back to their home country? Surely the Prince had influence over some lowly Spanish infidels.

The two men sat at a corner table watching a Spanish security officer at the door to the ramp. "Karim, we need to get out to the airplane or surely the prince will pay a hefty price."

"But Amir, how are we supposed to do that with the guard at the door. He seems very alert, and we can't just overpower him. We need to sneak out to the airplane, but how can we do that?"

"I don't know, Allah will show us the way."

Tim pulled the aircraft lighting system circuit breaker in the cockpit of the Gulfstream jet. He did not want the exterior, door and entry steps light coming on creating a potential problem to airport security. Backing out of the cockpit, he opened the door and gently lowered to stairway to the tarmac. Everything was wet. The heavy fog and mist created slippery surfaces on airplanes and the oil-soaked parking ramp. When Tim finally stood firmly on the tarmac, he listened, but heard nothing except for the hum of a distant building air handling system. He quickly closed the airplane door and moved to the landing gear of the neighboring Boeing jet. While unable to distinguish details, he could see the bulk of the large airplane parked just meters away from his position.

Both Arab bodyguards were beginning to panic and sweat profusely under their sport coats where small pistols were in concealed holsters behind each breast pocket. Spanish officials had earlier relieved them of their larger weapons but had not searched them out of deference to the prince. Karim tapped Amir on the arm and nodded toward the Executive Terminal Lounge entrance door. "Allah has been good to us. The cleaning crew is coming to do their work. That should cause some distraction for the guard. I will create an additional confusion to get the guard away from the door. When I do that, you will sneak out onto the ramp. I will remain here to await the prince."

Amir was uncomfortable. "What distraction will you do?"

"Wait and you will see. It will be a splendid distraction."

The gray metallic belly of the Boeing was shrouded in fog and dripping large beads of condensation. Tim, avoiding puddles of condensation on the tarmac, crept to the area between the main landing gear where he located the inspection panel. His night vision equipment gave a ghoulish, green cast to the fasteners holding the panel to the airframe. One-half turn on each of the sixteen fasteners and the panel was off. He checked his watch and noted he had only used thirty seconds to remove the panel. Not bad time for a pilot. He might even think about getting a maintenance job if things got slow. Surprisingly calm, he removed the small rectangular box from his pocket.

The box opened quietly and easily. He had practiced numerous times on the flight to Ibiza and had become quite proficient. Then he opened a second small box containing the blasting cap. He inserted the cap into the Semtex, connected the wires, closed the box, and set the arming switch. He stood, reached into the fuselage of the jet, and placed the device next to the center-line fuel tank and prepared to make his way back to the Directorate jet.

FIFTY-TWO

The tired airport cleaning crew shuffled into the Executive Terminal and began to unload equipment from their cart. Two women with the the haggard look of overworked, underpaid people all over the world began their routine tasks. They mostly looked at the floor and refused to make eye contact with anyone, especially the Spanish Security Officer at the door to the ramp. Seconds after the women began to sweep the floor and empty trash containers, Karim let out a gruesome, raspy scream, fell to the floor and started kicking, moaning, and jerking as if he were having a seizure. The cleaning women screamed and ran for the exit door, the Spanish Security Guard left his chair near the door and rushed to the writhing form on the floor. At that precise moment, Amir slipped out the door to the ramp and ran to where he thought the Boeing jet must be parked. He stumbled and lurched across the wet, uneven tarmac. Blinded by the pea-soup fog, he came up to a wet metallic shape, but soon discovered he was at the wrong airplane. He slipped on an oily patch, fell, scraped his knee and cursed loudly in his native tongue. He continued his search for the airplane but discovered he again had come upon the wrong aircraft. The irritated man cursed again as he moved toward his intended destination.

Tim had four more fasteners to tighten when he heard loud cursing in a foreign tongue. He could not determine the exact source of the voice, but he knew it was very near. Quickly, he finished fastening the panel and crouched against the left main landing gear straining for any sound. He thought the voice had come from the area of the next jet parked on the ramp but couldn't be certain. *Damn! My first op and this is what I get*, he thought silently to himself. His only weapon was a short screwdriver. He had no gun or knife, or any other mechanical or chemical means of defense. He heard wet shoes squishing on a wet surface a few seconds before he saw the faint form of a figure approach from his right. His night vision goggles provided an edge, and he intended to use it. The pitch-black night enhanced by the heavy fog and mist provided some cover. Through the mist, Tim could barely see the intruder. But the advancing individual wasn't looking at the landing gear, he was looking up at the airplane, probably trying to determine whether this was the right one. Tim decided to wait.

He held his breath and crouched motionless in the space behind and between the left main wheels trying to blend into the night. The individual stopped in front of the Boeing airplane, looked up, muttered something, and stood there like he was lost. He could not get into the airplane because there were no stairs up to the main door in the fuselage. The man began to walk toward the nose gear of the jet. If Tim could see the nose wheels, the intruder could see the main gear where Tim was partially concealed and cautiously fingering the screwdriver in his hand. Just as the man reached the tires, he stopped, turned and looked toward the terminal and away from Tim. The man stood under the nose of the plane trying to avoid the light drizzle that had just started.

Chaos in the Executive Terminal had run its course. Karim stopped writhing and screaming and assured the Spanish Security Guard no medical response was necessary. The Arab and the Guard exchanged words for several minutes. Finally, the Guard stopped questioning the man and went back to his chair by the door. A minute later, the Spaniard asked Karim, "Where is your associate?"

Karim shrugged, "Maybe he went to the rest room."

"Go get him. Bring him here now!" the guard demanded.

Karim walked slowly to the rest room, called for his partner, but no one answered. He turned, shrugged at the guard and sat on a nearby lounge chair.

Instantly, the guard became furious. He ordered the Arab to move to a metallic chair, then handcuffed him to it and made a hurried phone call. Seconds later, four heavily armed, angry Spanish Airport Police burst into the Executive Terminal through the door from the aircraft parking area. They spoke briefly with the Guard and ran back out through the door to their waiting vehicle.

Tim saw the blurred, but bright lights of a vehicle moving toward the Boeing from the Executive Terminal. He could see the man in front of the nosewheel of the jet as he stood erect and frozen in the approaching lights. Tim decided it was time for him to make his move. The roar of the approaching military vehicle, heavy fog and focus on the lone figure in the bright lights provided enough cover for Tim to run from under the Boeing back to the Gulfstream. While the police were busy with the man at the Boeing, Tim waited behind the left main wheels of the Gulfstream. When the truck drove away from the neighboring jet, Tim opened the aircraft door and climbed into the safety of the aircraft cabin. He dropped into one of the tan leather lounge chairs and sat there for a while.

FIFTY-THREE

A few hours after sunrise, the fog and mist lifted enough for the Directorate Gulfstream V to depart the Ibiza airport for the Azores. On Long Island, Control had successfully monitored the operation, a success thanks to hacks into airport security cameras and a United States satellite. Eddie had programmed the satellite to send its live signals to Control, and no one else. The signal disruption at NRO Headquarters was believed to be a technical problem that had eventually corrected itself. Satellite agency staff claimed aberrant sunspots caused signal anomalies, and that was the official reasoning for the signal interruption.

The center of interest at Control moved to Ron and Ingrid. Tail number HB-IZZ, a Boeing Business Jet was ready to depart Ibiza, Spain, for its destination, Geneva, Switzerland. The departure was only a few minutes into the future, a rather bleak future for the crew and passengers on the doomed aircraft.

Ron monitored Ibiza airport ground control radio.

"Ibiza Ground this is HB-IZZ. Ready for taxi with information Bravo."

"HB-IZZ. Ibiza Ground. You are cleared to taxi. Runway zero-six."

The aircraft taxied to the runway, changed to the Tower frequency and received clearance for take-off. After safely airborne, the black jet started a climbing left turn "on course to Flight Level Three Five Zero," also known as thirty-five thousand feet. Their departure into the bright, blue Mediterranean sky imitated the sea birds as they soared aloft looking for prey swimming in the brilliant, blue water below.

Ibiza radar monitored the departure as the jet climbed to cruise altitude.

Ron was listening to the voice traffic and watching the radar depiction directed to his computer screen by Eddie "the Hacker."

Ron calmly called out to the others in the room, "I show we have four minutes until detonation. Ingrid, Eddie are we still OK?"

Both replied. "Ready."

Exactly three minutes and fifty seconds later, the little white numbers denoting the Boeing jet disappeared from the radar screen. HB-IZZ no longer existed. Ron stood at his console and said to the group, "The device worked properly. In a few minutes we should start hearing radio traffic reporting an explosion, fire in the sky, debris falling into the ocean and general confusion." He sat down to listen to radio communications from several commercial aircraft alerting air traffic control of a fireball in the sky. Commercial and pleasure watercraft in the area of the explosion reported similar sightings. Air traffic control was trying to contact the stricken aircraft. Nothing to be done but recover survivors and debris. A US Navy helicopter in the area reported they were nearly struck by pieces of aircraft fuselage and wings falling from a fireball over their position. The debris field covered miles since the aircraft came apart at five hundred miles per hour and over thirty thousand feet above the calm waters of the Mediterranean. The Primary Director sent a message to the necessary parties lamenting the loss of a director and his staff. Kurt and Conrad walked out of the control room. Hugh and Cal met inside the courtyard in Aden, while Monsoor sipped wine in the house. Maybe a slight affront to Allah, maybe not.

FIFTY-FOUR

Three days later, the Long Island coast sported glorious weather, while inside the mansion, the group took their places around the conference table in the library. Kurt pressed a button and activated an electromagnetic field in the windows rendering them impervious to prying eyes, and sound and vibration detection devices. Conrad stood and addressed the group. "Our directors are extremely pleased with the stability that has returned to the group. Directorate leadership has been reinforced in the minds of any who might take a road separate from the common good. On another note, some of our assets are beginning to report additional threats from Al-Qaeda. We will begin examining our potential to identify and thwart these new dangers. Kurt has a few remarks. I must leave you for a few days. The directors have summoned me to an urgent meeting. Kurt and I thank you all for your work and the directors have asked me to deliver their thanks and appreciation to you. Each of you will find a more substantial reflection of their gratitude on your bank statements."

As soon as the automatic door closed behind Conrad, a wall panel disguised as a book-case slid to the side revealing a video screen. "Team, I would like to show you what our little operations have accomplished. Eddie was lucky enough to have hacked into some satellite traffic. Our government has finally acknowledged, and used, some of the information we supplied via our assets, by preventing planned attacks in Amman Jordan, and Los Angeles International Airport. The *USS Donovan* successfully completed their refueling stop at Aden. The explosives did not reach the target. Al Qaeda was able to retrieve the explosives but has not uncovered the real reason for the failure. The individual supplying the boat swears it was in perfect condition. Surprisingly, the hierarchy of Al-Qaeda believes one of their operatives has ties to the Russian government, but he cannot be located."

Eddie squirmed in his chair like a kid sitting at the dinner table with only the broccoli still staring at him from the plate. "Kurt, any news from Hugh?"

"His last transmission came from his chalet in the Swiss Alps. He loves to go there after a successful operation. I expect contact from him tonight. Now, if there is nothing else, I have some relatively urgent work. We will meet here for a working lunch."

What a week. Tim needed some rest and social diversion in his life. *What life? This job is my life. A change in scenery and time zones is necessary.* He decided to check his bank account and get that change of scenery.

Sitting in his room overlooking the ocean he became aware of how an ocean can appear a bit like life. One day the calm surface is a glorious blue, then in an instant it becomes angry and gray. Glorious, contented, cold, bleak, dangerous, foreboding, and just like a regular day at the office. But he was not at the office, and the world assumed a handsome appearance. Not beautiful like a frail, sensitive exterior, but a bold, magnificent, impressive character. Like the "presence" of a woman who can control a room full of men and women with just a glance or subtle movement. He had seen very few women like that, but there had been a few, and he never forgot the power and control they commanded.

He opened his computer to check his bank account balance. In the old days as a government employee, he would very carefully open the account, and sneak a peek hoping a positive balance would greet him, but not today. Since taking this job, his government retirement went into a domestic account that could be reviewed by any taxing agency from local to federal and would look like any other federal retiree. Then, after a few keystrokes a separate account appeared on the screen. He entered the proper information, sat back for an instant and let the computer do its magic.

The comment about the Swiss chalet had awakened a long dead, or repressed, interest. He always wanted a place in the mountains, and at the beach, and in the center of a thriving city like Paris or Rome. The balance in the account and the comments concerning Hugh prodded his mind to review various options. Between the signing bonus and the bonus from the latest operation, he already had enough money to get two of the three vacation options. In a few more months, the regular salary would cover the third location, and still provide enough for living expenses. His mind then took a turn to the past when as a newly employed Special Agent he worried about having enough money to pay bills and eat at the same time. Working for the government was not a road to immediate riches unless you were a politician. Saving the world was not a way to wealth. Saving people was not a road to untold prosperity unless the people owned or controlled most of the world. His reverie was broken by the little tone and a message on the computer screen asking if he wanted to continue the session. He signed out and broke the connection.

How would he use the money? He could not possibly use all of it for personal daily expenses because they were scant. The Directorate provided his food and lodging, and any spending for little niceties was a miniscule percentage of his wages. He had no relatives, no significant other, only his work. His life had not really changed at all, and now maybe it was time to do something about that.

FIFTY-FIVE

The senior Al Qaeda official sat at a worn and scratched old wooden table in the kitchen of his third house in the mountainous region known as Tora Bora in as many days. The Chechen was speaking on an encoded satellite phone, "Khallad, we have yet to determine the location of our man in Aden. He disappeared during the loading process at the dock that morning. Our people used GPS coordinates to pinpoint his cell phone. The phone seems to be at the Russian embassy. Our people working at the compound claim he is not there. We have reported sightings at different locations in Yemen, Saudi Arabia, Paris, London and Rome. He cannot be at any of those places, or I would have known. He is not in those places at the same time. I suspect he should have contacted me by now, but I have heard nothing."

Khallad interrupted the Chechen, "Unless he can divide himself into many parts, he is hiding in seclusion. Do you believe he has been captured by the Russians? I do not believe he has gone over to their side."

"Yes, he may be sitting in a Russian cell, but I doubt it. I do not believe my brother has erred. I spoke with him a few minutes before the package was delivered to the dock. He did not say anything was amiss. I will speak with the delivery people. Maybe he said something to them." The line went dead.

Normally a suspicious man, he did not share the positive thoughts of his Chechen associate. He had been at odds with them in the past. Thinking to himself, *I will wait for news, but will check other contacts. The Chechen is not infallible.* He dialed another number and waited for the connection. The persistent rings of satellite phone on a desk in a lavish apartment on the Persian Gulf fell upon deaf ears. He left no message.

The warm desert sun shone through the penthouse apartment of Prince bin Alkanoor. A secret panel in a piece of custom cabinetry was open revealing a full bar. Alcohol was not allowed in the principality, but most of the ruling class ignored that edict. Normally a contemplative man, not easily distracted, he could not concentrate on the solution to his problem. Early the previous evening, the family was notified by his associate that a Boeing Business Jet owned by his nephew had exploded and crashed into the Mediterranean Sea with no survivors. Even though the official recount of the incident claimed the cause was unknown, he was certain the Directorate had exacted its revenge on the young upstart. The arrogant fool thought he could successfully challenge these men with impunity. Now, Alkanor had to think about his future. He was certain he had been careful, but his nephew was another story. Three taps on the door broke his partial trance. He thought, *Who can that be knocking on my door. No one is allowed above the lobby unless they are a resident, or a resident gives permission for the person to come up. It must be another resident.* He checked the video security camera at his entrance door, and saw his neighbor, also a cousin, standing quietly, facing the camera. Alkanor relaxed; his cousin would be no threat. The man was his partner in the endeavor to take over control of the Directorate. He felt a bit confused. He did not expect to see his cousin at his door. They had agreed to avoid contact until after the initial shock of the incident had passed. He sighed, then opened the door and greeted the man. "As-salam-alaykum, my cousin."

"Wa-Alaikum-Salaam" came the reply from the man dressed in a white satin and gold robe denoting a member of the ruling royal family. "I have come to discuss our next move after the tragic death of your dear nephew."

Alkinor thought, *Yes, his death was tragic, but only because he failed in his mission to aid us in our plan.* "Please come in. I must admit I am surprised to see you here so soon. Do we have a problem?"

"I do not believe we have a problem at this time, but we must be very certain."

Alkanor could feel his anger rising, "I believe I understand your predicament, but we discussed this before we set out on the venture. We knew the young prince was a wild card, but you guaranteed he could be controlled. Apparently, that was not the case. You are a director. I am not. You have much to lose, but I am not in such a position. I am a mere prince, not a member of the royal line." He stopped short of saying more. He sensed he was very near a line he could not cross with this man.

The cousin stared steadily at Alkanor, "I detect a level of stress on your face. Do not fear, I have planned for this possibility. Our part in this will not be discovered. I guarantee it. Don't forget, we have their lifeblood, oil."

Alkanor visibly relaxed, "I understand. Now, what is our next step?"

"I must return to my apartment for a moment. I will return with details of our next move." He turned toward the door. "I will only be a moment."

Alkanor let out a deep breath and took in the view of the sparkling, deep blue waters of the gulf. He tried to calm his racing thoughts, but too many images flooded his head. The doorbell rang again. Out of habit, he shot a brief glance at the security camera video and saw the familiar image of his cousin in his royal robe. Seconds later he pulled open the door and immediately turned away to reach for his cell phone that had just started ringing. In the mild chaos of the moment caused by the doorbell and the ringing phone he paid no attention to the robed man entering his apartment. "Hello? Hello? Is anyone there?" The phone went dead, and so did Alkanor. While he had his back turned to the door, the man in the robe raised his silenced Beretta, Model 71, .22 caliber pistol with his gloved left hand and fired a single bullet into the right temple of Prince bin Alkanor. The high-speed projectile spun crazily inside the skull breaking into sharp shards of metal shredding brain tissue. Less than a minute later, the royal cousin, wearing surgical gloves, entered the unlocked apartment, placed a small pistol in the right hand of the body on the floor, dropped a spent shell casing and placed a suicide note on the bar next to a partially drained bottle of scotch whiskey. He stared at the prone figure of the late Alkanor and quietly said, "You will now fear no retribution. We three had a secret and now two are dead. Your secret is safe for all the ages." He returned to his apartment and the company of his grandson who wore the same white gold and silk of the royal family.

The intended recipient of the call, Prince bin Alkanor, could not answer the call. He could not, and would not, answer this or any other call. The warm desert sun shone brightly through the window upon the pale, lifeless face of a deceased prince. The official cause of death was listed as a suicide. A note on the table explained how the death of his beloved nephew, Prince Ibn Al-Wahidi, drove this man to end his life. The police, headed by a royal family member, accepted the physical evidence and suicide note at face value and closed the investigation. A lavish State Funeral was scheduled for a future date.

FIFTY-SIX

That afternoon, the Long Island kitchen staff laid out a fine prime rib buffet complete with mashed potatoes, creamed spinach, salads and breads. Tim thought it looked a lot like Lawry's Restaurant on Ontario Street in Chicago, but with much, much more physical security and genuine "Old World" elegance. Kurt joined the group for lunch, and small talk turned to potential outside activities like ball games, Broadway plays, bicycle tours, international travel and the like.

Kurt rose and raised the glass. "A toast from the directors to you for your fine work. 'To your continued success, health and wealth.'"

He lowered himself into his chair, and they all followed suit. "I will provide you with information concerning our next operation. Various groups are contemplating several actions that would have a tremendous impact on the directors. The outcomes of the actions are technically not a concern to their financial holdings, but control of those outcomes is a concern, much as winning or losing a war might have the same effect on wealth and power. Just because you lose a war does not necessarily result in poverty. The loser might receive new infrastructure that would create more wealth."

The door from the hallway quietly opened and Hugh appeared at the threshold. "I thought I would return a little early since a fast-moving Alpine-mountain storm was about to close the roads for a few days. Nice to see you all. Looks like I got back just in time for lunch and a movie." He winked at Ingrid and took a seat at the table.

Did Tim catch a fleeting unspoken message from Hugh to Ingrid? Was it acknowledged and returned? The ephemeral encounter lasted less than a second, but Tim was certain he had seen something.

Kurt sat emotionless at the table. The old Prussians would have been very proud. "Although our Aden and Ibiza Operations were successful, as well as our actions that foiled the Los Angeles and Amman threats, Al Qaeda appears to be rather steadfast in their desire to create havoc in the world. While we provided United States federal law enforcement and intelligence agencies with information concerning potential future attacks against New York, and the port of Aden, the directors have requested that we take no further direct action. They have instructed us to monitor our assets and sources, continue to interpret information, and provide them with our assessments. They will plan their economic decisions accordingly and will exercise their influence as necessary. They noted that sometimes conflict can be useful in proper amounts and situations to alleviate greater damage. Control can determine the outcome and the future. Sometimes a loss can be just as useful as a win. Besides, wins and losses are based upon the perspective of the players. The directors always increase their holdings and positions. They never lose."

FIFTY-SEVEN

The next night would be a Saturday night and Tim had not made any plans. He had not even thought of making plans. As usual, he was totally engrossed in his work. That was until he received a call on the in-house phone system.

The phone rang twice, Tim lifted the receiver and heard a familiar female voice. "Tim, this is Ingrid, are you busy?"

"No, I was contemplating absolutely nothing, and am about to go to the kitchen for a coffee."

"Would you mind if I joined you?"

"Of course not. I could use the company."

"Okay, see you in ten."

The phone went dead. Tim looked through the window at the ocean. Then it hit him. Ingrid had never spent any time with him or tried to talk with him other than what was necessary for the job. He was certain this was the interview with a shrink that Ron had told him about when he first came to the Directorate. He would be on guard for any "tricky" questions she might throw at him. He mentally put on his armor for protection from this probing shrink.

When Tim arrived, Ingrid was already seated at the small kitchen table. She lounged on a chair with her back to the wall while clasping a red ceramic mug filled with a dark, steaming brew. He filled a mug and sat across the table from the "inquiring mind" with whom he was ready to do battle.

"Hi, Tim. Thanks for joining me. I was about to go stir crazy. Are you becoming more comfortable with your new surroundings?"

"Yes, more and more every day. So much has happened. The hours are filled with work, there's little leisure time, the food is excellent, the view is terrific, and my bank account has never been so healthy. Everything seems to be working quite well. Yes, I believe my lot in life has changed for the better."

The woman smiled, cast her eyes down at her coffee mug, knitted her brow and softly said, "Tim you mentioned everything about your life here except for people and how you are managing on a personal, emotional level. No one should need to describe their life in strictly work and material terms. Before you say anything, let me say this. I am not asking you as a psychological profiler or as a professional. I am asking as a friend. I've seen your work, seen you interact with your peers and supervisors, and no one questions your work ethic or ability. I am asking because I want to know. I want to get to know you. Know you as a person."

Tim was stunned. He was not prepared for this. Unless she was very, very good at emotional warfare, this sounded like she truly wanted to become a friend. Tim had already realized the intricacies of meeting women compatible with his job. The potential was nearly nil. The large room seemed to shrink to the size of a table and two chairs with only two people. The bright lights seemed to dim, and his focus intensified on the woman seated across from him. Only now had he noticed her soft dark hair streaked with silver strands flowing to her shoulders, the refined nose, perfect lips and questioning gray eyes. He saw her as a woman, not a psychologist or associate. She had completely disarmed him. Then he caught himself. This was one hell of a good trick. He raised his lowered shield. "I would like to get to know you as well. We have been working together for some time now, and I just realized we have never spoken as friends, only as co-workers." Tim thought his response was sufficiently formal, trying to conceal his momentary mental and emotional weakness.

She leaned forward, her hand under her chin, her eyes fixed on his, "We should get together for a good talk before too long."

Tim was trying to extricate himself from this complicated moment, but his mind stumbled, and he could only come out with, "I 'm sorry, but I need to get back to my computer. I forgot to do some financial things that need to be done as soon as possible." Only minutes after he sat down at the kitchen table, he was rushing back to his sanctuary. He was unsettled, and he could not understand the feeling.

Ingrid sat startled trying to understand what had happened. Then she smiled to herself, "I guess I scared him. I wonder why?"

FIFTY-EIGHT

During the next several months, the team continued to work side-by-side in the Control Room on various projects. Avoidably, the USS Cole had been attacked and damaged by Al Qaeda in spite of warnings provided to the United States by the Directorate, and other attacks on Directorate assets and interests had been thwarted. Conrad convened a team meeting in the library and directed each member to take a few weeks off during the lull. He also directed them to travel away from the mansion, with the caveat that two members of the team remain on premises. Since their momentary meeting at the kitchen table a few months earlier, Tim had many encounters with Ingrid, but they never talked at length. Something always interfered, or Tim ran away. Despite those impediments, the psychologist had made her observations and arrived at a tentative plan to have her talk with the elusive Mr. Church.

When the vacation schedule was published, Ron and Tim were slated to be gone for the same two weeks, while Eddie and Hugh shared a time period and Ingrid had a solo slot. Tim looked forward to his time away from Long Island. Even "Paradise" could get tedious and boring, and he was ready for new sights, sounds and adventures, especially since he could now afford the good life. He chose Paris. The Directorate had access to several luxurious apartments in the best neighborhoods for Team members and he thought spring in Paris would be a great break. He also planned to look for an apartment for himself since he had accumulated enough funds to buy a very nice place.

Tim did not choose his destination. The destination chose him. Paris held fond memories for him, and the specific destination was necessary to those memories. He favored sitting at a window table enjoying the fare at the Maison de Hugo while watching the furs, fashion and jewels blend with young children, older couples and the world-weary as they weaved a human mosaic flowing past the canvass that is Paris. Quite idyllic. Of course, if the Maison de Hugo had no room, then the Romeo Bar and Grille across the Place Victor Hugo would do just fine. He could just imagine all the intrigue that had been hatched in this great city over the years, and it helped him reach that place in his mind where he could consider future options.

Warm breezes gently stirred smaller branches on the trees lining the boulevard while late afternoon road traffic settled to a trickle and sidewalks accommodated pedestrians rushing to their homes as the busy day melted into the soft evening. Tim sat at a small linen covered table enjoying a coffee and pastry when a voice jolted him into the present. Startled, he turned to see Ingrid standing beside his table.

"Hi, Tim, may I join you?"

THE END

About the Author

Retired local and federal law enforcement officer and US Air Force pilot and intelligence officer, the author, Mike Konyu, draws from his training and experience to create fictional accounts of actual incidents endangering the world. Years of conducting undercover, illegal arms trafficking and complex domestic and foreign crime investigations laced with intelligence gathering operations provide a foundation for his stories and characters. He now resides with his wife, Judith, in an active retirement community near Chandler, Arizona.

Made in the USA
Columbia, SC
05 March 2023